Treasure of the Jaguar King

J. A. Johnson

an
Evanation Studios
Production

DEDICATION

For my son, Evan

CONTENTS

ACKNOWLEDGMENTS

Thanks to my good friend, author K. G. McAbee, for keeping me on my game.

PROLOGUE

1901 A.D.
   Nicaduras, The Temple of the Jaguar King

The fer-de-lance, that deadliest of snakes of the Americas, had taken Julia, and there had been nothing to do but leave her lifeless body to the jungle.

Martin Conrad sobbed as he hacked his way through the undergrowth. After ten expeditions how could it have all gone so horribly wrong now that they were so close?

He thought about little Adam and was torn between pressing on and turning back. But giving up would not guarantee his safe return home to his young son in Mar Azul. Indeed, all the peril they had endured thus far would still be waiting to try and claim him once again on the return trip.

If he turned back now, all would have been for naught.

Julia.

He owed it to Julia to press on, to claim the treasure that had cost them so much already.

He had the map. There was still a chance.

Resolved to continue the quest, he stopped to rest and to consult the map once again. He shucked off his haversack which still bristled with toxic darts. *Damn the savages*, he thought. It had been while fleeing the Yanaro warriors, with all caution thrown to the wind, that he and Julia had encountered the fer-de-lance.

Exactly when the warriors had given up the chase and why, he couldn't say except that it had seemed to coincide with the thickening of the jungle.

Martin wiped the sweat and tears from his eyes as he drew out the rolled leather map and spread it upon the trunk of a fallen tree. The map was old, the leather supple and paper thin.

Based upon their trip upriver, before the hail of arrows had forced them to abandon their canoe, he had a reasonable idea as to where he was now. Consulting his compass, Martin set his course to the Northwest. He repacked his belongings, hefted his machete and cautiously resumed his terrible quest.

With every step, the terrain became steeper, until at length, Martin's only progress was made by climbing. Finding purchase on root, and rock, and vine, he scaled the increasingly sheer slope. At last he reached the summit. Before him sprawled an unnaturally flat mountain plateau. Few trees grew upon it. Almost at once, in spite of the concealing cover of lush grasses and flowering bushes, Martin knew that he was standing amid the ruins of an ancient city; a lost city. He felt several things at once; vindication, elation, but more than these, he felt misery, even guilt. This was no ordinary 'lost' city. This was the near mythical, *City of the Jaguar King;* the city he and Julia had spent years searching for. And now he stood here triumphant while, Julia, poor Julia, lay dead in the jungle.

He suppressed his misery as something in the distance caught his eye; something he had only been able to imagine until now. He had been staring blankly ahead, beyond the ruins, to where the mountain beyond the plateau towered above the remains of the lost city, its upper reaches cloaked by a mantle of perpetual cloud cover.

It was an awe inspiring backdrop for an awe inspiring sight. Standing near a small, mist-shrouded lake, was a great, stepped pyramid, at least three time taller than any yet discovered and, atop it...

The Temple of the Jaguar King!

****

As Martin hurried toward the pyramid a sudden, uncanny darkness, a shadowy gloom, fell across the plateau. He drew up short. The veil of clouds that concealed the mountain's peak appeared unchanged. And yet...

The faint rumblings of thunder rose up around him. An approaching storm?

The temple ruins. He could shelter there. He quickly covered the remaining distance to the base of the pyramid. He stopped and regarded the stone steps that led up to the temple proper, which sat perched upon the towering pyramid's flat top.

So many steps. He doubted that he had the energy left to reach the top. If the coming storm brought with it lightning, he would be fully exposed with no where to run.

As scanned the structure for some other point if ingress, the thunder grew louder. More than that though, it no longer sounded like thunder.

Martin swallowed uneasily. His breathing became quick and shallow. He knew that sound, and in this place of all places it was terrifying in the extreme.

He knew now that he would never even set eyes upon the treasure he had sacrificed so much to claim. It would remain lost, here in this most cursed of places, while he would soon be with Julia once again.

There was no thunder; no storm. There was only the a ruined city and the ruined lives of those who sought its greatest treasure.

He whimpered under his breath, and slowly turned. He wondered what would become of little Adam.

1
MAR AZUL

1922 A.D.

Mar Azul, Nicaduras

Mar Azul. *Blue Sea*. Whoever had christened the small river town with such a name had had a sense of humor to be sure; that, or they had been near-sighted and color blind. For one thing, the ocean was three day's boat ride away. For another thing, there was nothing blue about Mar Azul except the sky. There was only the emerald green jungle and the sanguine river, tinted as it was by the red earth through which it flowed.

Father Harmon Kirby sat beneath the thatched awning of *Anaconda* hotel and stared blankly at the downpour obscuring his view of the river. He was pondering his imminent foray into Nicadura's mountainous interior. In his mid-fifties and not-particularly athletic, he was beginning to think that he was too old to continue the expeditions; that maybe this one would be his last. After all, it had been twenty years and ten expeditions, hadn't it? No one could say he hadn't he tried?

He shifted his attention to the dregs of his warm beer. He sighed, turned the dirty mug up and polished off its contents in a single gulp. He set the empty mug down on the weathered old table and, as if in reply, the rain slackened to a drizzle.

All down the muddy slope to the lazily flowing *Rio Lagarto*, people seemed to pop up like mushrooms, resuming activities put temporarily on hold by the downpour. Men bustled among the long, heavily burdened banana boats that lay beached like whales on the riverbank. Bundle by bundle, they proceeded to transfer their cargo of green bananas to the steamer anchored along Mar Azul's steep riverbank, for transport down river and, from there, to ports around the world.

The sound of laughing children drew Father Kirby's attention down the riverbank, past several thatch roofed houses that stood well above the river on deceptively tenuous looking stilt-legs. Half a dozen bronze children emerged from the foliage under the houses. He smiled as they darted to the nearest untended boat and proceeded to help themselves to as many bananas as they could carry. Dropping as much fruit as not, the little buggers scampered back up the riverbank and melted into the shadows beneath the houses.

Well, if nothing else had been accomplished during his midday *refreshment*, Father Kirby now had a theme for the afternoon's lesson. *Sin and Penance*. He dropped a few coins on the table and headed for the door.

Manuel, the bartender, rearranging the smudges on the drinking glasses with a dirty rag, acknowledged his departure with a lift of his sparsely whiskered chin. "Padre."

At the door, Father Kirby took his ratty old cappello hat and umbrella from their wall peg. He perched his hat upon his curly red head, stepped out into the waning drizzle, and decided to use the umbrella as a walking stick. The beads of his Rosary clicked and rustled together as as he strode the plank walkway up the hill toward the *Our Lady of the River Orphanage*

The orphanage was Father Kirby's pride and joy.

Twenty-five years ago, and straight out of the seminary, when he had first been assigned to Mar Azul and its environs, he could hardly contain his excitement. The place was so unlike Brooklyn where he had grown up, as to be an alien world. But that was exactly what thrilled him.

The Sister had met him at the boat's gangplank when he had first arrived and, seeing the happiness writ large on his face, greeted him with two words. "Six months."

"I'm sorry, what?"

She had taken the larger of his two suitcases and set off toward the string of buildings further up the river bank. "They say it takes six months for the novelty to wear off a new place. After six months you'll know if you really love it, or if you loathe it."

"Oh, I'm not worried about that," he had replied as they stepped onto the hard packed trail that ran parallel to the river.

The nun had shrugged. "We'll see." She had looked back at him without slowing. "By the way, I'm Sister Mary-Agnes."

The 'novelty' of Mar Azul had faded by the end of the first week. And though he never had, and never would, admit it to Sister Mary-Agnes, it had taken considerably more than six mons for Father Kirby to not completely loathe Mar Azul: the heat, the humidity, the vampire-like mosquitoes, the snakes, the crocodiles, and let's not forget, the jaguars, had all taken their toll upon his enthusiasm.

While he might never have come to *completely* loathe Mar Azul, he might never have come to truly love the place had he not found more purpose here than merely his duties as a priest. He vividly recalled the fateful day when a naked, half-starved child, delirious with fever, came floating down the river in a dugout canoe. No one knew where she had come from or who her people were.

Some thought that the child spoke some sort of dialect; that there where hints of various Nicaduran language groups in her speech. Father Kirby, however, was eventually convinced that the child had spoken an entirely different language.

Whatever the case, the little girl had been able to convey her name. And because she had acquired both English and Spanish with frightful ease, the motivation to learn her language had evaporated as quickly the morning mists on the river.

The child's name was, Atziri.

The closet thing to a clue as to who she was and where she came from, was Atziri herself or, rather, the tattoo on her forehead. Yet, as clues went, it never bore any fruit since no one had been able to ascribe any meaning to it.

There had been much speculation, of course. The most outlandish theory being that she was, Yanaro. The quasi mythical, completely terrifying Jaguar People, who killed for pleasure, ate the living hearts of their enemies, and spread misfortune like a plague to all who encountered them.

That theory alone had effectively ruled out reuniting the girl with her people. For the Yanaro supposedly lived in the wildest, most remote, most inhospitable region of Nicaduras, and no one in Mar Azul had been willing to trek into that hellhole just to return a half starved child to a notorious tribe that apparently did not want her in the first place. Especially if the reward for doing so might well be having to watch one's own heart being eaten before one's very eyes.

In short order, Father Kirby and Sister Mary-Agnes had found themselves with a renewed purpose. And so the *Our Lady of the River Orphanage* had come into being.

That had been twenty years ago.

It was also the same year that Martin and Julia Conrad arrived in Mar Azul claiming to be Protestant missionaries.

Would that that had been the truth.

2

ONE LAST EXPEDITION

The Conrads had trekked up river an astonishing half a dozen times that first year, until Julia had become pregnant. And it wasn't until their son had been born the following year, that Father Kirby learned that the Conrads weren't missionaries, of any denominational stripe whatsoever.

In fact, they weren't even Protestants. They were as Catholic as Father Kirby himself. Aside from lecturing them about missing Mass and the Blessed Sacrament for nearly a year, Father Kirby had reminded them of their need for Reconciliation. "Confession being good for the Soul, as they say."

The Conrads had offered no details about their business in the upriver wilds, and Father Kirby had decided not to press them on the subject.

****

By the time, Adam Johnathan Conrad had been born, Martin and Julia had become upstanding members of the little river Parish. Needless to say the Conrads had become regulars at Mass. That was, at least, until Julia was fit enough to resume their inland expeditions.

It was then, on the last day that Father Kirby was to ever see the Conrads again, that he had learned the truth about why they had settled in Mar Azul.

He was awakened that fateful day by, Sister Mary-Agnes pounding on his door.

"Yes, yes, Sister! What is all the ruckus about?" he had demanded, being unable to think of a single reason for being roused from his hammock at such an ungodly hour.

"They're leaving!" she exclaimed with tears in her eyes.

Father Kirby dressed quickly and, lantern in hand, headed for the riverbank. Sure enough the Conrads were there loading their boat. But they weren't 'leaving' as Sister Mary-Agnes feared. Father Kirby knew as much at a glance. He had seen the Conrads prepping for their mysterious inland forays enough times recognize what they were up to on this occasion.

The only difference this time had been Adam. Nested in a coil of rope in the bottom of the boat, the baby had been wholly preoccupied with his toes while his parents busied themselves loading their bundled supplies.

Surely to God they were not intent on dragging the boy along with them? Father Kirby recalled thinking. "What in Heaven's name do you think you're doing?" He demanded.

"Oh! Good morning, Father," Julia had beamed.

"Father," echoed Martin.

Father Kirby had held the lantern high enough to illuminate both Martin's and Julia's faces at the same time. "Answer my question, Martin. What do you think you're doing?"

****

Later, on the Anaconda's veranda, as the morning sun tinted pink the sky in the East, Father Kirby almost spit out his coffee. "You're damned fools, the both of you!" When neither Martin nor Julia replied, he went on. "When I learned that you weren't missionaries, roaming the untamed Nicaduran wilds in search of souls to save, I never pressed you about your affairs. I assumed that you had a good reason, and that you'd share it with me in due time. But, but..." he shook his head in disbelief. "But the *Treasure of the Jaguar King*?"

Martin frowned. "You don't believe it's real?"

"For the love of the Lord in Heaven. It. Is. A. *Myth.*"

Martin glanced at Julia who reciprocated with a subtle nod. Martin reached into his shirt and produced a rolled piece of leather. He slipped the thong that bound it and spread it out upon the table. A map.

Father Kirby stared at it, recognized a few of the landmarks near the lower edge.

"It's old," said Julia.

Father Kirby felt an uneasiness welling in his gut. "How old?"

Martin smiled. "Very old."

"You don't know?"

"We had several antiquaries look at it," Julia said as she placed her hand upon the supple leather map, practically caressing the thing. "They all agreed to between 800 and a 1,000 years.

Father Kirby continued to stare at the leather map. His first impression had been that the hieroglyphs and depiction of Nicaduras had been painted. But paint would not have survived so long on a map so old. For a moment, he thought that maybe the image had been applied with a stain, but even as he thought so, he ruled the idea out.

"Is the image... is it a tattoo?" he asked.

The Conrads nodded and Father Kirby felt nauseous. He could feel the corruption coiling off the map like an invisible smoke, polluting the very air they breathed. With some effort, he refrained from signing the Cross for fear that by doing so would shift the focus.

"How did you come to possess this, *map*?" he asked.

"It belonged to my father," Martin had said. "He was a coffee importer. How he acquired it, he never said. In fact he had never mentioned it. After he passed away, I came across it while going through his things."

More than a few questions danced through Father Kirby's mind, but before he could ask any of them, Martin continued.

"The map itself would have been little more than a curiosity had it not been included in a folio of notes; notes that revealed the map to be of Nicaudras."

Father Kirby nodded. "And your Father, how did he die?"

"Slowly," Julia interjected. "He fell ill with a fever, here in Nicaduras, while looking for the treasure. The illness became debilitating, sapping him of energy and, ultimately, the will to live."

Martin looked weary. "Fortunately, he was home in Michigan when he left this life."

****

They had sat quietly sipping their lukewarm coffees while the sun crested the treetops on the other side of the river. At length, Father Kirby said, "Even though I am of the mind that the *Treasure of the Jaguar King* is a myth, I suppose I can understand your coming here given your family's history with this map. But," and he held up an admonishing finger, "you are parents now. You have too much too lose, risking your lives in these godforsaken jungles chasing a treasure." He had turned his finger to point at Adam, cradled in Julia's arms. "That baby boy, is the only treasure that should matter to you. He is real and he needs his parents."

Both Martin and Julia looked chastened and, for a moment, Father Kirby believed that he had gotten through to them, that they had come to their senses.

He was mistaken.

"Believe us," Martin had begun. "We know the dangers, the risks."

Julia had lifted little Adam up and set him upon the table before her. She kissed him playfully before turning serious. "Father, we are broke. We're penniless."

Father Kirby looked questioningly at Martin. "The family coffee import business?"

A look of desperation clouded Martin's expression. "Squandered. My best guess is that my father either spent his fortune acquiring the map, or spent it looking for the treasure."

Sensing another opportunity dissuade the Conrads from their foolish and dangerous ambition, Father Kirby affected a frown. "If chasing this treasure cost your father the family fortune, not to mention his life, how do propose to succeed where he failed if you have no money?"

Martin looked at his infant son. "What choice do we have?"

Father Kirby had looked at the map spread before them. How could he dissuade them? "That map is evil," he said. "And if the *Treasure of the Jaguar King* is real, then it is no less evil."

Julia set Adam back in her lap. "It's only one last expedition, Father. Before we departed, we were going to speak to you; to ask you and the Sisters to watch over Adam until we returned."

It was as if they had not heard a thing he had said.

3

THE MOONFLOWER

1922 A.D.
  Mar Azul, Nicaduras

In typical fashion, the rain had ended as quickly as it had come upon them. The jungle began to buzz and chirp and hiss as the wildlife, like the people of the sleepy river town, resumed the daily business of living.

Adam Conrad had only to wait a short while before resuming his own task. When it was completed, he sloshed out of the rust colored river and turned back to admire his handiwork. "Well, I wouldn't call it art," he confessed.

"It doesn't matter, as long as you spelled it correctly," replied the young woman from under the awning that shaded the last third of the old steamer.

Adam did a quick double-check of the word he had painted in black on the hull near the bow. M. O. O. N. F. L. O. W. E. R. "Nah, I'm good," he said. He dropped the brush into his small paint can and moved up the bank to the narrow wooden gangplank that bridged the gap between the 30-foot vessel and the red clay soil at the water's edge.

As he crossed over and boarded the boat, he smiled at Atziri, after whom he had christened the steamer. She sat on the low bench, sipping naranjada, an orange juice drink she had bought at the Anaconda. She was feeding chunks of banana to Jasper, his, or rather her, pet Capuchin monkey. Like her short white dress, Atziri's sky blue *huipil* blouse, decorated with a two-headed eagle and serpents, stood in stark contrast to her long, coal black hair which, today, she wore loose and parted in the middle in such a way that it hid most of the tattoo that he found so beguiling.

Adam returned her smile as he sat down next to her. He set the can of paint on the upturned crate they were using as a makeshift table, and let down the legs of his khaki trousers which had been rolled up past his knees for wading.

Atziri handed him her glass. He sipped from it, enjoying the sweetened, though still slightly bitter, orange drink.

"It's very exciting," she began. "All the children in the orphanage are talking about your boat."

"Our boat," Adam corrected her. "We're partners, remember?"

"Our boat," she said. "And Jasper's, too." She handed the monkey the last of the fruit.

Sometimes, when Atziri talked about the children and the orphanage, it was easy to forget that neither of them were wards there anymore, or that Atziri now worked there alongside Father Kirby and Sister Mary-Agnes.

"So, what do the children say?" he asked.

Atziri smiled. "Different things. "Little Tepin believes you will bring him treats every time you return from the coast. Patli is sure that you will sail away to become a river pirate. And, of course, Itzama thinks that you will sail up river to find treasure."

Adam pushed his wide brimmed Panama hat further back on his head. "Tepin might be right about the treats. Patli, well, he's the only one in Mar Azul with the temperament for piracy. Thankfully he's only seven. Now, Itzama," Adam began as he slowly leaned over the crate and looked deep into the obsidian pools of Atziri's thickly lashed eyes. "If Itzama, knew anything about treasure, he would know that the only treasure worth wanting is right here in Mar Azul."

Atziri met his gaze. "And what manner of treasure can a poor river town like Mar Azul possibly offer?"

Adam gave her a roguish grin. "Oh, I think we both know the answer to that," he said as he slowly leaned closer to kiss her.

Something wet met Adam's lips. He straightened and touched his mouth. His fingers came away black.

Jasper chittered and chirped and waved Adam's paintbrush in the air.

Atziri burst out laughing.

"Jaaaasper!" Adam reached for the little monkey, but it was already abounding away down the gunwale toward the gangplank.

"Let him go," Atziri said. She plucked the hand rag from Adam's back pocket and proceeded to wipe the paint from his face.

"When exactly did you steal my monkey?" Adam asked.

"Our monkey," Atziri teased. "We're partners, remember?"

The sound of a steam whistle caused them both to look up. Another steamer, a good bit larger than the *Moonflower's* 30-feet, was puffing upriver. Adam recognized the familiar boat at once. "*la Tortuga.*"

"Has it been two years already?" Atziri asked.

"I guess so," Adam replied as they both waved from beneath the awning.

Captain Fenton and the crew of *la Tortuga* came to Mar Azul every other year and, with Father Kirby to lead them, they traveled into the interior to spread the Good News among the indigenous tribes.

"Ahoy, there!" Called an unshaven man from the bow of *la Tortuga*. Captain Charles Fenton.

As *la Tortuga* steamed by, Fenton removed his skipper's cap and bowed. "What a beautiful lady you have there, Adam!"

Adam smiled proudly and patted the cool boiler of the *Moonflower*. "Thanks Captain! I just bought her two weeks ago."

"Not the boat, my boy," Fenton hollered as *la Tortuga* slowly carried him past the *Moonflower*. "Tubs like her are as common as leaves in the jungle. No, I was referring to Atziri. I do believe she gets lovelier every time I see her."

4
THE CREW OF LA TORTUGA

Adam fiddled with the *Moonflower's* boiler for no real reason. There was nothing more to be done to the steamer. Nothing more that could be done until the new replacement valve arrived from *Cabo de Sol.* The sun was setting low above the jungle. Over the rising buzz of insects, the squawks, hoots, and howls of animals filled the thick, humid air. He looked back toward the *Our Lady of the River Orphanage* but there was no sign of Atziri, Father Kirby, or Sister Mary-Agnes.

He looked the other way, to the far end of the riverfront town, and found the Anaconda hotel spilling light and noise into the darkening night. The crew of *la Tortuga* was no doubt at the center of the excitement.

Just then, Jasper came scampering up the gangplank, a bow tied around his neck. The little monkey perched upon the gunwale near Adam and proceeded pick at the red bow, chittering irritably. "Not my problem, buddy. That's what you get for letting a woman dress you." The Capuchin squeaked and tried to chew the bow. "You should have stayed here with me," Adam said. "Look at me, I'm wearing the same clothes I've worn all day."

It occurred to Adam that maybe he should have changed into something else. He glanced down at his white linen shirt, loose fitting and comfortable, his tan, khaki pants which he wore tucked into the tops of his high leather boots; boots that he wore as some measure of protection against snakes. "I reckon I'm presentable. What say you, Jasper?"

The monkey, with both hands and one foot now engaged with the offensive bow, ignored him.

The sound of voices brought Adam's attention back to the orphanage. *Finally*, he thought when he saw Atziri, Father Kirby, and Sister Mary-Agnes heading his way.

Adam picked up his hat and perched it atop his head. "Alright, Jasper, let's go," he said as he scooped up the frustrated monkey and perched him upon his shoulder. "And, Jasper, remember your table manners."

The monkey chirped excitedly.

"And how are things with your boat, Adam?" Father Kirby asked as they gathered at the foot of the gangplank.

Adam gestured over his shoulder. "Oh, you know, nothing that a new valve and a Blessing can't fix."

The priest nodded. "Well, I can't help you with the valve, but a blessing, now that's specialty."

"Maybe later, Father," Sister Mary-Agnes interjected before the priest could begin. "We shouldn't keep Captain Fenton and the others waiting."

Father Kirby arched an eyebrow. "Are you saying I'm long winded now?" Adam noticed Father Kirby wink at Atziri. "Jesus, Mary, and Joseph, it's like I'm married, I tell you."

Atziri grinned as the priest and the nun continued along the worn dirt path toward the Anaconda.

"May I," Adam grinned as he offered Atziri his arm. She looked beautiful as always. She wore the same white dress as before, but had changed into her other *huipil* blouse; the red one, with a Yellow and white floral design woven into it. She now wore her hair in a single, thick braid draped forward over one shoulder and tied with a length of the same red ribbon she had evidently used to make Jasper's bow.

****

Mar Azul had few amenities to offer river travelers, but everything it did offer could be found in one place. The Anaconda hotel. Thatch roofed and unpainted, it was the largest structure in Mar Azul fronting the *Rio Lagarto*. A wide veranda snaked from one end of the Anaconda to the other and on it, was an assortment of tables and chairs in various states of dilapidation.

The Anaconda was a restaurant that few ever ate at, a hotel that even fewer ever roomed in. It was also a tavern. In the latter capacity, the Anaconda had no shortage of patronage. It even boasted an old billiard table.

"Adam! Atziri!" cried Manuel, the Anaconda's owner, as they entered. The little proprietor, who typically moved with all the urgency of a sloth, and who almost never smiled was like a new person. Of course, the arrival of Captain Fenton and the crew of *la Tortuga*, was generally Manuel's busiest day of the year, bi-annually speaking. "Come in! Come in!" he said.

Upon seeing them enter, Captain Fenton leapt to his feet and motioned them to two conspicuously empty chairs at the Anaconda's largest table. He pulled out one chair for Atziri. "My, my, my," he said to her. "I swear, if young Adam here hasn't married you by the next time I visit, I will propose to you myself."

Atziri blushed.

"Captain Fenton, you will do no such thing," said Sister Mary-Agnes.

Fenton looked at Adam. "Whose to say?"

Adam never could tell when the riverboat captain was serious or when he was just having fun at his and Sister Mary-Agnes' expense. It was no secret how Adam felt about Atziri. That he would one day ask to marry her was a given, in his mind anyway. But the *Moonflower* was a necessary first part of that equation, without which a proposal would have to wait.

As for the matronly Sister Mary-Agnes, Atziri was like a daughter. Had been from the day Atziri had drifted downriver to Mar Azul, a half dead child in an old canoe. A child they say that no one had wanted to take in because of the strange, birdlike language she had spoken and the mysterious, unreadable tattoo that framed her forehead.

"*Yanaro,*" they had whispered, filling the word with fear and superstition. "*Yanaro.*"

5

DINNER AT THE ANACONDA

The aromatic scent of Captain Fenton's pipe smoke vied for prominence within the Anaconda, competing with the smell of *Pepián de Pollo;* the traditional, spicy chicken stew that was Manuel's specialty and a favorite of the crew of *la Tortuga.*

As Manuel made the rounds, ladling out second helpings of the stew, Captain Fenton hitched his pipe toward the thin man seated next to him. "Ed Matthis here is an artist."

Adam nodded to the gaunt, bespectacled man. "I noticed the sketch book," he said, though in fact what he had noticed most about the man, was his fixation on Atziri. "You've been drawing in it throughout the meal."

"My apologies if I seem rude," said the man. "I have the habit of sketching things of beauty. Capturing them in time if you will."

Adam felt his jaw tense.

"Like a photograph," Father Kirby said hastily.

Matthis literally snorted. "A photograph is a soulless, lifeless thing, Father."

The priest nodded. "That, and I suppose the jungle is rather harsh on cameras and film."

Captain Fenton laughed and slapped the tabletop. "Precisely right, Padre. Our sponsor, Mr. Hect. insisted on Matthis joining us for just that reason. You see, last year, I led another expedition up a tributary of the *Rio Blanca* in Guatemala. After we got back, we found that all of the film we had shot had been ruined by moisture. An absolute waste. To say that Mr. Hect was not pleased would be putting it mildly."

Adam frowned. "Can't sketch books be ruined as well?"

Matthis' brow furrowed in annoyance. "What would you have us do, chisel pictographs on stone tablets? If my sketches suffer damage, I will know it *long* before we depart the jungle. I can redraw them if need be."

"You must be quite talented, to compete with a camera," Adam prodded.

"Care to judge for yourself?" Matthis said smugly as he handed the large, leather bound sketch book across the table.

Adam ignored Jasper as the curious monkey dropped from the rafters to investigate. Adam tried to hold his expression in check as he looked at Matthis' work. The man was extremely talented indeed. On the left page were several quick sketches, the *Moonflower*, the Anaconda, even Father Kirby and Sister Mary-Agnes walking along the riverbank. The sketches were all better than anything, Adam himself could ever hope to aspire to. But it was the right page that struck him the most. There, occupying the entire page, was a drawing of Atziri. A portrait so detailed that, had he not known better, Adam might have first mistaken to be a photograph.

"Oh my," said Atziri, as she leaned closer to see for herself. "That's amazing, Mr. Matthis. It's like looking into a mirror."

Jasper chittered as though in agreement.

The artist smiled and nodded. "You may keep it, if you like."

"Thank you," she replied.

Adam noticed the joy in Atziri's face. It was the first time he had ever felt jealous about her. Adam forced himself to smile. "It seems your sponsor has an eye for talent, Mr. Matthis."

Matthis took the sketch book back and carefully tore the page out. He handed it to Atziri, who then passed it to Sister Mary-Agnes and Father Kirby to look at.

Jasper followed the paper and Adam half hoped that the Capuchin would snatch it up and run away with it. But, for once, the monkey actually behaved himself.

Sister Mary-Agnes held the drawing up next to Atziri's face. "He even captured your tattoo perfectly," she said.

The artist took a sip from his glass of water. "It is a most curious design," he said. "Does it have a meaning?"

Atziri's copper cheeks darkened a shade with self consciousnesses. "I don't know to be honest. I've had it for as long as I can remember."

"But surely, somebody knows. A family member?"

Atziri indicated Adam, Father Kirby, and Sister Mary-Agnes with a wave of her hand. "This is my family."

Matthis sat up straighter, exuding more curiosity than seemed warranted to Adam. "What about your tribesmen?"

The last of the happy glow faded from Atziri's eyes. "I don't have a tribe. I was..."

Father Kirby cleared his throat. "We found Atziri drifting downriver in an old dugout canoe, naked as the day she was born, feverish and half starved. She might have four or five years old at the time, but we can only guess."

Sister Mary-Agnes handed the drawing back to Atziri. "That was two decades ago, nearly a year after Adam's parents went missing. That was a difficult period to say the least. But I like to think that some good grew out of it." She looked at Adam and Atziri. "These two are the reason Father and I established the *Our Lady of the River Orphanage*."

"That's nice," Matthis said somewhat perfunctorily.

"You seem disappointed," Adam said.

"Hmm? No. Not all," the artist replied. "Its just that I have a keen interest in the indigenous peoples of the region. The idea that you might be from a heretofore unknown people is an exciting prospect."

"People used to say that I was, Yanaro," Atziri offered.

Matthis shook his head. "I've never heard of them."

"I have," said another of the crew, a Nicaduran man named Villatoro, who was unfamiliar to Adam. "There's no such tribe. The Yanaro are a myth. Ghost story stuff told to frighten children. My own *abuela* used to scare my *hermanos* and me whenever we misbehaved. *'You wicked children'*, she would say, *'if you don't behave the Yanaro will come and take you away. And if they don't feed you to the jaguars, they will eat you themselves.'"*

Atziri looked uneasy and Sister Mary-Agnes said, "We will have no more such talk."

Captain Fenton glared at the man. "You have insulted my friends, Chano" he said gruffly. "I believe an apology is in order."

Chano Villatoro's eyes flicked briefly in Atziri's. "I am very sorry, miss, if I..."

Atziri smiled. "I am not offended. Whether or not the Yanaro are real does not matter to me. My people, my 'tribe', are here in Mar Azul." She placed her hand atop Adam's and his irritation with Edward Matthis melted away... enough, at any rate.

Manuel then brought out a traditional Nicaduran dessert of bananas in vanilla sauce. "Manuel!" cried Captain Fenton. "First your fantastic *Pepián de Pollo* and now, *Bananos En Leche*! You should leave Mar Azul and open a fancy *restaurante* in *Cabo de Sol*. You could become a wealthy man indeed."

Manuel bowed and retreated to the kitchen, beaming with pride.

The awkwardness of the previous conversation faded then, and talk turned to the missionary expedition. Captain Fenton sent one of his crew, a fellow named Thompson, to *la Tortuga* to fetch his map. When the man returned, Fenton cleared an area of the table and spread the map out. Everyone crowded around as the steamer captain began detailing their intended route into the interior and the known villages they hoped to visit.

Finally, Father Kirby consulted the pocket watch which, alongside his rosary, hung from the sash he wore around the waist of his cassock. "Nine o'clock," he announced. "If we are to leave at dawn, I suggest we turn in for the night."

6

LA TORTUGA DEPARTS

On such cloudless nights, there was nowhere for the moon to hide. It shown down from above like an all seeing eye, dispelling shadows with its pale blue radiance; revealing prey and predator alike. It projected itself upon the face of the *Rio Lagarto*, piercing the surface and probing the depths where piranhas swarmed and crocodiles lie in ambush.

The moonlight sought out open windows and spilled its tourmaline glow upon a wide awake, Adam Conrad. From beneath the mosquito netting around his bed, Adam stared out of his window and into the radiant night. He listened to the insects drone their atonal chorus, but it was neither the brightness of the night, nor the cacophony of the rain forest's denizens that kept him awake. It was thinking about the coming dawn and Father Kirby's missionary trip into the Nicaduran interior that made him restless.

Adam had only asked once to accompany Father and the others and he had, thankfully, been told no. He had been twelve years old at the time and he had only asked then because he thought that if he didn't at least appear interested, they might suspect the truth, that he was afraid of the jungle.

It had been the jungle that had taken his parents, swallowed them up with utter indifference. For years he had wondered how they might have died and his youthful imagination had conceived no end of horrible possibilities.

But now, now his childhood fear of the jungle had been supplanted by a rational apprehension. He could think of no worthwhile reason to venture into the heart of such a dangerous and deadly domain. He understood Father Kirby's motivation as a man of the cloth. Yet, heading toward sixty, Father Kirby was not exactly in the best physical shape for such an adventure.

Adam's struggle now, was that he himself was no longer a child, too young to trek deep into the jungle. He knew that he should join the missionary trip inland if, for no other reason than to look after Father Kirby's safety. And yet, Adam's fear of the jungle held him back. He felt guilty and tried to convince himself that Fenton and his crew were seasoned experts, and that he would just be in the way if he imposed himself upon their expedition.

Finally the moon moved on, darkness reclaimed his room, and the Mar Azul night fell silent. Adam slipped into a restless sleep. He dreamed of jaguars with glowing, hellish eyes; of dark impenetrable jungles, thick with shadows and the weight of death.

He was awakened, hours later, by the sound of voices down by the river.

****

The stars above the eastern horizon were melting into the reddening sky in advance of the rising sun. Adam dressed hastily and was still stepping into his boots as he hurried from his bungalow, toward the riverbank were *la Tortuga* was anchored.

In the dawning light, he saw the dark shapes of Atziri and Sister Mary-Agnes approaching from from the direction of the *Our Lady of the River Orphanage*. Atziri waved upon seeing him. He waved and waited for the women to join him.

"I thought I'd over slept," he explained as they made their way together down the hard packed footpath.

On the riverbank, near the foot of the gangplank, were a few boxes, labeled 'Bibles', which Simon McHenry and Cal Thompson were transferring to *la Tortuga*. On the boat, Ed Matthis was securing his bundled art supplies near the bow. While amidships, their guide, Chano Villatoro, leaned indifferently against the gunwale, watching the sunrise and smoking a cigar.

Captain Fenton nodded to Adam. "I was beginning to think you weren't going to make it. I had half a mind to send Chano to fetch you." The Nicaduran flicked the remains of his cigar into the river. He scoffed at Fenton's joke. "I am your guide and nothing more, señor. You would be wise to remember that."

Father Kirby, in the stern, took charge of the boxes of Bibles as they were brought aboard and stowed them under the bench seats along the inner hull. As the last box was put in its place, the priest looked up and smiled, apparently only just noticing Adam, Atziri, and Sister Mary-Agnes.

"Ah, good, good, you're all here," he said. Never one for lengthy farewells, Father Kirby turned to Fenton. "Are we ready for the blessing? After all, I suggest we get underway before it gets overly hot."

The captain removed his cap and turned to the other men on the boat. "You heard the Padre."

The men bowed their heads, as did Adam and the two women.

Father Kirby cleared his throat and made the Sign of the Cross. "Lord, as we embark upon this journey up treacherous waterways, through tangled and dangerous jungle, plagued with the threat of fevers and hounded by deadly creatures, we call upon you to make safe our path, to help us in this our undertaking, and to deliver us safely home again. In the name of the Father, and of the Son, and of the Holy Spirit. Amen."

If Father Kirby had been trying to pile stones upon Adam's guilt, he couldn't have done a better job.

Fenton donned his cap and gestured to Adam. "If you're inclined to join us, lad, now is the time."

Adam smiled sheepishly. How ironic, he thought, that the first time he didn't want to join them, they finally invited him. He gestured over his should to where the *Moonflower* rested at anchor. "I know I've pestered you for the chance to go in the past, but I really want to get the *Moonflower* running as soon as possible."

Captain Fenton nodded. "I know the feeling, Adam."

Sister Mary-Agnes stepped to very edge of the water. "Father Kirby, did you bring your umbrella?"

Even in the rosy light of the dawn, Father Harmon Kirby looked embarrassed. "Yes, yes," he replied tersely.

"Well, you be sure to use it. You remember what happened the last time. You came back as pink as a boiled shrimp."

Atziri raised a hand to her lips to cover her smile. Adam tried not to laugh, recalling the brilliant pink visage of the priest.

The moment had lightened Adam's mood considerably as the gangplank was drawn up and the anchor hoisted. He was still smiling as *la Tortuga* steamed upriver... to meet its fate.

7

THE WAITING

In the five weeks since Father Kirby and the crew of *la Tortuga* had set out on their bi-annual missionary expedition, little had happened in the river town of Mar Azul. So little in fact, that Adam had taken to spending most of his days onboard the *Moonflower*. Today was no exception. He lolled in the hammock he had strung up beneath the *Moonflower's* awning, and enjoyed the gentle swaying created as the steamer rocked softly in the current. Yet, as comfortable as he appeared, the truth was quite the contrary.

He had been expecting the replacement gauge for the *Moonflower's* boiler to arrive even before *la Tortuga* had departed. And like the overdue gauge, Father Kirby's expedition was now overdue as well.

Adam knew that a week late wasn't long enough to truly begin to worry, but a sense of foreboding had settle on him like a dense, sticky fog. He could not shake the feeling that he should have gone with them.

Stop it, he admonished himself. *Be patient. Everything will be fine.* He turned his attention to the book in his hands, *This Side of Paradise*, by an author he had never heard of named, F. Scott Fitzgerald. He flipped through to the page where he had left off and began to read. After a page, he lost focus, his attention drawn like a magnet, back to the overdue expedition.

He closed the book and tucked it next to him in the hammock. The air, as always, was think and humid. Before long, he yawned and, shortly thereafter was fast asleep.

****

"It's here! It's here! The part, Adam, it's here!"

He sat up so fast that he almost tumbled out of the hammock. He squinted as his eyes adjusted to the glare of the afternoon sun. Atziri, was running down the path, waving a small box. Jasper bounded past her, reaching the *Moonflower* a moment before Atziri.

Aboard the small steamer, Atziri smiled as she tried to catch her breath. She handed Adam the package. He glanced at the address. *Abner & Sons Steam Works, Cincinnati, Ohio.* "Finally!"

"I told you," Atziri said. She leaned close as he proceeded to tear away the brown paper wrapping.

Adam smiled at her as the last of the packaging fell away. "You've been telling me everyday. You were bound to be right eventually."

He held up the gauge and examined it, thankful that it was indeed the correct one. He retrieved his toolbox from its place near the firewood bin.

Atziri crouched next Adam as he set to work removing the old gauge. "Is there something I can do?" she asked.

"Guard the toolbox."

Atziri blinked. "What do you mean guard the... Oh," she said as she saw Jasper creeping toward the open box, one hand extended for a quick snatch and run. "No you don't, you rascal," she warned. The monkey froze. Then, with a series of angry squeaks, he sprang onto the nearby bench where he sat sulking to the extent that a monkey could do so.

"There," Adam said as he tightened the last screw.

Atziri looked surprised. "That's it?"

"That's it." Adam kissed her on the cheek. He tossed his wrenches and the old gauge into the tool box. He then shut and secured the lid against a certain thieving monkey.

"Let's go for a ride," Atziri beamed.

Adam agreed. "My thoughts exactly." He he raised the gangplank, and returned it to its hooks on the side of the hull. He added several pieces of firewood to the firebox and lit them. He and Atziri watched the gauges, the new one in particular, as the head of steam slowly built. Nearly half an hour later, the engine came alive, puttering rhythmically like a mechanical heart.

Adam stood ready with the long pole, while Atziri move quickly to the windlass, just as they had practiced many an afternoon, and soon she had the anchor hoisted. Adam braced the long pole upon the riverbank as Atziri moved aft to the tiller. Together, they directed the *Moonflower* out into deeper water.

****

For a while, Jasper scampered and bounced around the boat, exploring it as though it was something entirely new. Eventually, he settled onto a bench, leaned over the gunwale, and watched the river flow past.

For a time, they kept closer to Mar Azul where there was plenty of river traffic, mostly canoes and long, sleek banana boats. They waved at a passing steam boat. "That's our competition," Adam commented.

Atziri watched the other steamer continue on downriver. "I think there is enough business for all of us," she said optimistically.

Adam agreed, even though they had never completely decided what exactly their business would entail. At times they talked of delivering bananas to the coast, at other times delivering mail, and still at other times, ferrying people up and down the *Rio Lagarto*. Adam had more or less accepted that likelihood that it would be some combination of the those things.

They steamed up the river, until Mar Azul was well out of sight. Along the riverside, they saw the occasional, thatch roofed home with laundry strung up on sagging clotheslines and where children and chickens roamed yards of packed earth and tall grass.

In the shallows, fishermen stood casting their nets. They waved as the *Moonflower* chuffed by.

Adam fed more wood into the firebox and checked his gauges. He returned to his seat at the tiller and Atziri settled next to him, her head on his shoulder.

Neither spoke for a time, but then Atziri said, "You're very quiet, Adam. Is something wrong?"

"I'm just think about Father Kirby and the others."

"He has been late before. You remember one time he was two and a half weeks late," she reminded him.

He hadn't forgotten. On that occasion, six years ago, *la Tortuga* had run afoul of a sunken tree. The props had been damaged. Captain Fenton had been forced to stop for days to affect repairs as best he could. The additional days had understandably reduced their food supply. They had been forced inland on foot to hunt. It had then taken many more days to limp back to Mar Azul.

Adam sighed. "You're right."

Atziri smiled up at him. "Aren't I always right?" she teased.

He kissed her again. "I reckon we've gone far enough. Let's head home."

A steered the *Moonflower* in a wide arc and headed downriver for Mar Azul. In an effort to contain his concern for his friends, Adam said, "What do you say tomorrow we head for Cabo de Sol to see if we can find any work?"

Atziri sat up straight. "Are you sure? That's six days, round trip."

"Sure. Why not? We have to start somewhere, sometime. Unless, of course..."

"No, no, I agree. It's business, but it will be like a vacation too."

Adam nodded. "What about Sister Mary-Agnes?"

"I know she'll be shorthanded at the orphanage, but she has Sister Joan to help her. Besides, I don't actually do anything important."

Adam waved off her comments. "I know that, but I wasn't thinking about the orphanage. Aside from the fact that she is a nun, you're like a daughter to her and we are not married."

Atziri frowned. "And whose fault is that?"

They had had this conversation many times before but this was not a day that Adam wanted to ruin with that old debate. "I'm going to blame it on the gauge."

Atziri's expression suddenly brightened. "I have an idea! We could get married in Cabo de Sol!"

"You know we can't do that," Adam said as he steered the *Moonflower* around a floating tree limb. "When we get married, we'll be married by Father Kirby."

Atziri folded her arms and slumped back against the hull. "You're right, I know."

"We don't have to go scrounge work in Cabo de Sol right away. It's not like we're up against a deadline or anything."

"No." Atziri replied flatly. "I love Mar Azul as much as you do, but I need a change of scenery."

Adam understood the feeling. "So we're back to the same question. What about Sister Mary-Agnes?"

"Don't worry. I can handle Sister Mary-Agnes."

"And if she doesn't listen to you?"

"I'm a grown woman. But if it makes her feel any better, we can always take a chaperone."

"A what? Who?" Adam demanded, feeling almost defeated already.

Atziri scooped up the little monkey who had come down from the awning to examine the tiller. "Why, Jasper of course!"

8

THE CORPSE

Even from a distance, they could see that something unusual was happening in Mar Azul. A throng of people large enough to be most of the town was gathered at the water's edge.

"Say, what do you suppose s going on?" Adam said as he steered the *Moonflower* towards her usual place along the riverbank. His sudden dread was a cold, steel ball in his gut.

Atziri, with Jasper clinging to her shoulder, moved to the bow for both a better look and to prepare to drop the anchor. "I can't tell, but whatever it is, it looks to be something in the water."

Adam shut the throttle and the engine stopped turning. He then put the boiler in standing mode; just in case. In case if what, he couldn't say. The anchor splashed into the ochre current. The steamboat drifted backwards a few feet before the chain drew taught and brought her to a stop. Adam hastily positioned the gangplank between the boat and the bank and Atziri followed him ashore.

The gathered villagers were huddled close together, murmuring excitedly. Then, from out the gaggle dark heads and straw hats, Adam saw the familiar wimple of Sister Mary-Agnes as she stood straight to look around. Seeing Adam and Atziri, she broke from the crowd and hurried to meet them.

"Oh, thank goodness you're here," she said. "No one knows what to do."

"Why? What is it?" Adam asked as the nun whisked him and Atziri along. "What are you talking about?"

"Come, see for yourself," said Sister Mary-Agnes.

The three of them hurried the remaining distance. The crowd, as though sensing their approach parted before them.

There, in the dense tangle of tall grass the choking the shallows, was dugout canoe. It looked old, and unremarkable with one notable exception: a peculiar 'split' bow. There was something vaguely familiar about the small craft, but Adam was already focused on the occupant. A man, an Indian, dressed in a jaguar hide waist cloth, his hair adorned with iridescent, green quetzal feathers. A man with dried blood caked around his mouth and nose, who's unresponsive eyes stared blankly at the noonday sun. A man who was undeniably dead.

Atziri gasped and looked away.

The fear that the people had been attracted by something related to Father Kirby came and went, but then... Adam took the hand-rag from his back pocket and cover his mouth and nose against the smell of rotting flesh. He moved closer to the Indian, fought down the urge to vomit. There was something vaguely familiar in the gruesome remains of the face.

Adam swallowed uneasily. He drew a deep breath through the rag before using the cloth to wipe the paint and dried blood from the dead man's face.

"It's Chano Villatoro," he said in recognition. And then Adam gasped. Across the corpse's forehead, was painted an all too familiar design.

Adam turned to Atziri. She had overcome her initial revulsion and, though pale and queasy looking, she was staring at Villatoro's face. Adam met her uneasy gaze as her eyes shifted to meet his. Villatoro's forehead had been painted with the same design as Atziri's forehead tattoo.

"Yanaro," someone said.

"Yanaro," echoed another, and then the entire gathering was repeating the word in superstitious tones. Several people took renewed notice of Atziri. She turned and raced up the riverbank toward the *Our Lady of the River Orphanage.*

Sister Mary-Agnes turned her troubled eyes briefly upon Adam before hurrying after Atziri.

Adam turned back to the macabre scene of the dugout canoe. He noticed Manuel standing among the crowd. "He's not Yanaro," he assured the villagers. He looked to Manuel. "You don't recognize him, Manuel? He was one of Captain Fenton's men."

The owner of the Anaconda hotel regarded the dead man with some trepidation. "Si," was all he said.

Satisfied, Adam said, "Help me get him ashore."

Reluctantly, Manuel and two other men helped Adam drag the canoe clear of the river; no one made any effort to lay hold of the body.

Several entangled thoughts swirled through Adam's mind. The simplest question being, why was Villatoro dressed as an Indian? The second question was, considering all of the hundreds of miles of twisting, turning rivers, what were the odds that this man, dressed in this manner, and with a newly applied tattoo just like Atziri's, would was ashore in Mar Azul of all places.

None of it could be coincidental.

Adam noticed the oar still held fast in one of Villatoro's dead hands. "He was the expedition's guide. He would have known the way back," he thought aloud.

"I think he has not been dead very long, Señor Conrad," Manuel observed.

"But what killed him?"

Adam looked at Manuel and the others. There were no police in Mar Azul, no authority to handle a situation such as this. Normally, Father Kirby was entrusted to handle anything out of the ordinary. But now... well, Father Kirby's whereabouts and fate were unknown so, whatever was to be done in this situation fell to them.

"If we want to find out," Adam said, "we're going to have to get him out of the canoe."

Manuel looked uneasy. The other two men backed away, no longer wanting any part of the affair.

"Fine," Adam said, exasperated. He hesitantly took hold of Chano Villatoro's corpse and lifted it from the canoe. The Oar fell away, clattered in the bottom of the wooden boat. Villatoro's head tipped forward, coming to rest against Adam's chest and shoulder. The feathered headdress, tumbled away.

"Señor, look!" Manuel pointed to the back of the dead man's neck.

A dark, slender dart, perhaps ten inched long, protruded from Villatoro's neck, near the base of his skull.

"Poison dart." Adam gently laid the body on the grassy slope and carefully extracted the deadly projectile. He did not recognize the workmanship.

Manuel seemed on the verge of commenting, but Adam interrupted him. "Don't say it, Manuel. Not every unknown thing is Yanaro."

Just as he was wondering if Chano Villatoro had been the victim an Indian attack, or of deliberate murder, Adam noticed something in the boat where the dead body had been been sitting. "Eh? What's this?" he said to know one in particular.

It was a bundle of fabric. Villatoro's clothing. With growing certainty, Adam felt the tribal warrior disguise was exactly that, a disguise meant to assist his return to civilization.

Adam picked up the bundle and felt something wrapped inside. Curious, he peeled away the clothing and his heart seized tight in his chest. Wrapped in the garments was Father Kirby's personal Bible. Adam's legs felt weak. He wanted to sit down.

There was no way that the kindly old priest would willingly part with his Bible. Had Father Kirby died in the jungle? Had Villatoro died bringing the Holy Book back?

Father Harmon Kirby had been the closest thing Adam had ever had to a father. And he thought that he might cry. He stared at the old, well-used book. He ran his trembling hand over the leather cover. Saw that other papers had been stuffed among the pages.

Slowly, almost reverently, he opened the weighty tome and received yet another surprise.

The book was not a Bible. It was journal; a record of expeditions past, filled with handwritten notes, sketches, maps, and even dried, flattened plant specimens.

Adam closed the book. "Manuel, see to it that this man gets buried." Then, without another word, he hurried up the slope toward the *Our Lady of the River Orphanage*.

9
A BOOK OF SECRETS

Jasper sat on the window sill of Father Kirby's office at the rear of the orphanage. The curious Capuchin monkey sat frozen, staring intently at a large Harlequin Beetle as the enormous insect crawled slowly up the wall. After a moment, the monkey hopped over to the cluttered desk in a single bound, snatched up a pencil, and leaped back to the sill.

"Jasper," said Adam. "Bring that back, I'm using it."

The little monkey ignored him, as usual, and proceeded to prod the indifferent insect with the pencil.

"You've ruined my monkey," Adam said resignedly to Atziri.

He sighed and the room fell into silence.

Adam, Atziri, and Sister Mary-Agnes sat around Father Kirby's desk. Spread before them like a patchwork tablecloth, were dozens of papers; everything from notes written on scraps of material, to loose pages densely covered in Father Kirby's familiar handwriting, to maps detailing heretofore unfamiliar regions of the Nicaduran wilderness.

There was the occasional tattered photograph of Father Kirby, Captain Fenton, random members of Fenton's various crews, as well as Indians of varied tribes; some familiar, some not.

And then, perhaps most importantly, there was the journal disguised as Father Kirby's personal Bible. The actual Bible being currently tucked away among the books on the shelf behind Sister Mary-Agnes. The journal was a detailed chronicle of every trip Father Kirby had undertaken in the years following the disappearance of Adam's parents, two decades before.

None of the journeys had been missionary in the least. Not even one.

The lengthiest, most intensive of the expeditions had been the first; undertaken when there was at least some a glimmer of hope for finding Adam's parents, or at least some hard, physical clues as to their plight. Every other year thereafter, the expeditions had become more inquisitive in nature, pressing further and further into the interior with each attempt, contacting as many tribes as possible, in the hope that someone, somewhere, might know something about Martin and Julia Conrad's fate.

Adam and the two women poured over the journal entries and the related miscellany, piecing together a history of hardship, perseverance, heartache, and faith upon the part of Father Harmon Kirby. Adam was touched to learn of the priest's dedication to his parents and, as a result, he felt an even greater appreciation toward the holy man for raising him as a son.

There was no question in Adam's mind, but that he should take the *Moonflower* inland in search of Father Kirby. For if there was even a chance that the old priest was still alive, Adam owed it to the man to try and save him.

Resolved to what he must do, Adam dove into the last of the journal entries, eager for any information that might aid him in his plans. But what he read left him stunned, his mind reeling.

"Did you know?" he asked Sister Mary-Agnes.

The nun looked as bewildered as he felt. "I had no idea? I always believed the trips were mission trips. Father never even hinted otherwise. I... I..." she shook her head as though still letting the truth sink in.

Next to Adam, Atziri was staring so intently at a drawing she held in her hands as to stare right through it. Adam reached over and gently laid a hand upon hers. "Atziri?"

She turned her dark eyes toward his. "It's the same. They were there," she said flatly.

Adam took the drawing signed by Ed Matthis. It was dated three weeks ago. The highly detailed drawing was of a stone stelae, a human-jaguar hybrid, half hidden in the undergrowth and a blanket of creepers. Emblazoned upon the forehead of the savage, stone face, was a tattoo identical to Atziri's.

"My people," she whispered. "They found them."

Sister Mary-Agnes stood, and stepped to the window, that looked upriver, in the direction of the mysterious depths of Nicacuras' primal heart. After a moment, she looked at Adam. "Do you think they found it? The treasure, I mean?"

Adam's gaze drifted to the spread of documents on the desk before him. Sometime, after the second expedition seeking clues to his parent's fate, the focus of the expeditions had become as much a quest for the *Treasure of the Jaguar King* as for his parents. According to Father Kirby's journal, he had come to believe that Adam's parents had indeed located the lost kingdom of the Jaguar King and the people who lived there, the Yanaro. He believed too that the two things; his parent's fate and the treasure's location were inextricably linked; that to find one was to find the other.

"I don't know," Adam admitted. "But if the trails of my parents and Father Kirby end where the treasure lies, I mean to seek it out myself."

Sister Mary-Agnes turned to face him. "The treasure?"

"Adam frowned. "Damn the treasure. If it exists, it's cursed. It's already taken from me more than money can replace."

Adam pointed to the map. "This is a copy," he observed.

Atziri peeled her attention away from the drawing of the Yanaro stelae and regarded the map. "How can you know?"

"All of the writing is in Father Kirby's hand," Adam said. "See? He has dates written along the different rivers. They correspond to the journal entries. But see?" He tapped the most recent date. "The dates end here, but the map continues in some detail. It should be blank, unless someone had charted it before."

Atziri nodded slowly. "Then we should hope it is a good map."

Adam regarded her with a sense of dread. "What do you mean *we*?"

Atziri, held up Matthis' drawing of the stelae. "I'm going with you."

Jasper tossed the pencil out the window, bounded across the desktop and took up his perch upon Atziri's shoulder. He chirped sharply as though seconding Atziri's assertion.

10
UP THE RIO LAGARTO

The *Moonflower* floated at anchor, awash in the orange glow of the dawning day. Perched upon her bow, half a dozen keen-billed toucans croaked like frogs as though planning the day ahead.

The large-beaked birds fell silent as Adam approached the steamer. Then, just a he reached the gangplank, Jasper darted between his feet, nearly tripping him. As the monkey scampered toward the front of the boat, the toucans issued a chorus of angry, coughing squawks. The loitering flock then took to the air, and Adam watched them as they flew low over the face of the river, then banked clumsily toward the nearby trees.

Atziri joined him, carrying a haversack of her own. "For a moment, I thought we were taking on passengers," she joked as she handed him her belongings. Adam smiled and set the haversack next to his on the bench by the tiller. The rest of the supplies and provisions they needed were already stowed about the boat.

Adam worked quickly, firing up the boiler but it would take at least twenty minutes to build up sufficient steam to get underway.

The voices of excited children carried down the sloping bank to them. They turned and found Sister Mary-Agnes headed their way with what looked to be all eleven children from the orphanage in her wake.

"Come on, before this gets complicated," Adam said quietly to Atziri.

"Don't be like that," she said. "Sister means well. She's very sweet."

"Still..." said Adam as he impatiently regarded his gauges.

****

Sister Mary-Agnes stopped in the tall grass at the foot of the gangplank. The curious children jabbered like the toucans before them. "Quiet, children. Quiet." said the nun. "This is important."

"Good morning, Sister," Adam said warmly.

The matronly nun sighed heavily as though steeling her resolve. "I suppose there is nothing more I can say to change your minds?"

Adam could see the anguish in her kindly eyes; that she had been crying was evident from the redness and the puffiness around them. "Sister, Father Kirby might..."

Sister Mary-Agnes held up a silencing hand. "I know, I know, I know," she conceded. "I just can't bear the thought of losing you two to the jungle as well. But I understand. And to be honest, I don't blame you. I would search for him too, if I were younger."

"We'll be careful," Atziri assured her.

Sister Mary-Agnes looked down at her left hand. Only then did Adam notice the cloth-wrapped bundle. Catching his gaze, the nun said, "You should have this. I have a feeling you're going to need it."

Adam stepped down the gangplank and she handed it to him. To his surprise, the object was quite heavy, the fabric oily. "What is it?" he asked as he began to unwrap it.

"It's one of your father's pistols."

A gasp of collective awe escaped the children as Adam slid the old Army Colt from the leather holster that had been wrapped up with it. The pistol had been well cared for and it glinted coldly in the light of the rising sun.

He holstered the pistol and buckled the belt around his waist.

"Here, it won't be of much use without these," said Sister Mary-Agnes. She handed him a beaten looking box of bullets. "There aren't many – I counted twenty-five – but it's better than nothing."

Adam was speechless. He fumbled for something to say. "Sister, I..."

"If you have everything you need, I suggest you get going while the day is young." There was a faint tremor in her voice, but Sister

Mary-Agnes maintained her composure. "I'll be praying for you all, Harmon and the others included."

Atziri crowded close to Adam on the narrow gangplank and then hopped to the riverbank. She gave Sister Mary-Agnes a hug. "Like I said, we'll be careful. I promise."

Adam smiled gratefully and re-boarded the *Moonflower*.

****

El Rio Lagarto, the Lizard River, stretched westward, twisting and turning, narrowing and widening, snaking its way out of the mysterious, emerald green heart of the Nicaduran jungle.

With its flat bottom and shallow draft, the *Moonflower* could navigate all but the shallowest of places. Even so, Adam was constantly alert for obstacles, reading the river as best he could for hidden dangers such as rocks, shallows, and sandbars to name a but few.

Adam felt the easy breeze rustling the brim of his hat. The open air of the river always felt cooler to him than the steaming embrace of the jungle. He enjoyed it now, imaging the time when he and Atziri would spend their days ferrying goods and people up and down river for a living. It was hardly a grand ambition, but it was a life together. Of course it wasn't quite that simple. The mountainous, mist-shrouded Nicaduran interior held them both captives of their pasts, and neither of them were able, or even entirely willing, to break free.

Lost in such thoughts, Adam had said little as the *Moonflower* chuffed its way up river. Atziri too, had been quiet. She sat at the tiller next to him. Her hair pulled back in a long ponytail. She was holding Matthis' drawing of the Yanaro stelae, staring had the frightful stone visage.

It was a remarkable piece of art, but Adam was confident that Atziri saw nothing of it beyond the stylized symbol on the stelae's forehead: a mysterious symbol that looked just like the tattoo on her own forehead.

It could not be a coincidence. Somehow it was all connected; the disappearance of his parents, the disappearance of Father Kirby and the crew of *la Tortuga*; mystery of Atziri's unknown origins; the possible existence of the quasi mythical Yanaro, and of course, the fabled *Treasure of the Jaguar King*. How it all fit together and what it all meant, was something the answer to which lay somewhere in the dark, primordial heart of Nicaduras.

11
MYTH NO MORE

The *Moonflower* was anchored some fifty yards up a tributary of the *Rio Lagarto*. Overhead, the shadow-heavy canopy hid the steamer from the moon, the stars, and the scudding, gray clouds.

The air vibrated softly with the droning of insects. And all around the thirty-foot launch, fireflies swarmed in an aimless, blinking ballet. The languid surface of the tributary glittered with their glowing reflections. And in the black-as-pitch reaches of the surrounding jungle, a hundred prowling deaths were betrayed by eyes of burning amber.

Adam put the boiler in standing mode and, with one hand draped upon the butt of his revolver, stared out into that darkness with no small measure of respect. Finally he turned to Atziri just as she finished stringing up the mosquito net up around the *Moonflower's* awning. Adam nodded approvingly. "At least we won't be eaten alive by insects."

They settled in under the awning where a large candle burned softly, just strong enough to push back the night around them. Jasper sat on the starboard bench nibbling a bit of fruit that Atziri had prepared for him. Between bites, the Capuchin glanced nervously through the net and the into the raucous, jungle night.

"Here," Atziri said. She handed Adam a carved wooden plate as he sat down next to her. "I sliced us some *níspero*."

"Thanks," Adam said as he took a piece of the apple-like fruit and ate it.

From one of several boxes under the tiller bench, Atziri brought forth a few strips of dried meat to round out their simple meal. Adam glimpsed several cans of beans, and pretended he didn't notice. Beans would be his food of last resort.

They ate in uncharacteristic silence for some time. Finally, Atziri said, "Do you think Father Kirby is still alive?"

"I... I don't know," he said honestly. "We can only hope and pray." The idea of Father Kirby disappearing as his parents had, with no definitive answer as to their fate, was a torturous thought; one he would rather not consider until he had no choice.

"Do you think he found the treasure your parents had looked for?"

"The *Treasure of the Jaguar King*. I don't know. It's possible I suppose."

"If he did, do you think it means they found the lost city?"

Adam was taken aback by Atziri's sudden barrage of questions. It was like listening to the kids from the orphanage peppering him with questions while he had been refitting the *Moonflower*. And then it occurred to him where the questions were leading.

He looked at her and smiled gently. "You mean did they find the Yanaro?"

Atziri nodded, her eyes both hopeful and fearful. "They must be real," she said. She slipped the Matthis drawing out from under her blue *huipil* blouse and unfolded it. "If they didn't find the lost city, I think they were very, very close."

A jaguar roared in the darkness and a cold chill slithered up Adam's spine. Atziri moved close to him. Jasper tossed the last bit of fruit aside and sprang into Atziri's lap.

"We should get some sleep," Adam said.

He pulled a blanket from the under the port side bench and the three of them laid down in the bottom of the boat. He blew out the lantern. Atziri laid her head on his shoulder; the floral scent of her hair soothed his unease. Even so, he rested his other hand on the revolver, and listened to the jungle.

****

When Adam woke, the world was as gray as a photograph. The dawning sun had not yet picked its way through the jungle canopy. Upon the nearby riverbank, misty tendrils curled and coiled like snakes around root and vine. The vapors flowed and rolled, converged upon the river from both banks. They spilled out over the water like a spectral veil.

During the restless night, Adam had kept the boiler at the ready. And now he proceeded to add wood to the furnace, building steam for their departure. He extended the gangplank and they went briefly ashore to relieve themselves. Even the monkey made use of the opportunity.

After a quick breakfast of boiled eggs and dried plantains, they were underway once again. Soon, Adam had the *Moonflower* back on the *Rio Lagarto*, heading upriver.

The boat traffic had lessened considerably, now that Mar Azul was well behind them. They saw the occasional fisherman out for his daily catch. They passed a banana boat bound for the coast with its green cargo. It wasn't until midday that the boat traffic became worthy of notice.

Adam saw the three dugout canoes approaching them from upriver. Even from a distance, he could see that they were indians; their brilliant, green quetzal feathers gleaming in the noonday sun.

Atziri noticed them at nearly the same moment. "Look how they're dressed," she whispered.

Adam had already taken notice. The six indians, two to a canoe, were dressed just as Chano Villatoro had been when they had found him dead in a similar craft.

Yanaro. He thought the word now with a dreadful, absolute certainty.

Adam held the tiller steady, his right hand hovering near to the holstered revolver, as the dugouts began to pass them on the port side. The indians said nothing, but their painted faces turned as one. Adam saw their eyes widen as though struck by some sudden, unexpected surprise.

They seemed not to notice him at all, their rapt gazes transfixed by Atziri.

And just like that, the boats were behind them.

But just as Adam began to feel a sense of relief, he glanced back again and saw the three dugout canoes turning around.

The Yanaro were coming back.

12
RIVER FIGHT

Adam hurriedly added wood to the furnace, building steam. The three Yanaro dugouts were relatively short, each perhaps eight to ten feet long. The Yanaros worked their paddles furiously but, turning the canoes cost them valuable time and widened the distance between them and the *Moonflower*.

"Can they catch us?" Atziri asked worriedly.

Adam looked back. "I doubt it. They're paddling upriver. They'll tire and slow down."

They both watched as the canoes began to slowly narrow the gap between them.

"Are you sure?" Atziri said.

Adam winced. "Sort of."

"That wasn't the answer I was hoping for."

The *Rio Lagarto* appeared calm, but the current was deceptively strong. Adam regarded the three canoes for several moments. Was it his imagination or were they finally beginning to slow? Had their initial burst of speed sapped them so quickly? He stared a moment more and realized that while they were no longer gaining, they were not falling behind either. They were pacing themselves. He wasn't about to say as much to Atziri but, because he still believed that the Yanaro would tire eventually, he grinned and said, "See? They're tiring already. While we, on the other hand, have plenty of firewood. We're not about to tire or slow down."

Atziri sighed heavily, clearly relieved, which made the half-truth worth it in his opinion. It was then that the first poison dart zipped between them. It struck the boiler and ricocheted over the port side of the steamer where it splashed into the river.

"Get down!" Adam said as he ducked below the gunwale, pulling Atziri down with him. He risked a glance forward, assured himself that the way ahead was clear. "Hold the tiller steady."

Atziri laid hold of the tiller as another poison dart whisked by, this one lodging itself in the side of the firewood box amidship. The her eyes widened.

"Japser! Come here! Come here, boy!" Atziri pleaded. The Capuchin monkey, oblivious to their predicament, was up in the stern, snooping around their stowed camping gear.

A third dart slammed into one of the uprights supporting the awning.

"Jasper!" she yelled.

The monkey turned toward her only to be startled by a fourth dart as it penetrated crate upin which he sat. In a flash, Jasper was at Atziri's side.

Adam drew his father's revolver and checked the rounds in its cylinder.

"You're not really going to shoot them are you?"

Adam gestured at the pistol in his hand. "That's sort of the point, don't you think?"

"But you've never killed anyone before."

Adam pointed to the long, needle-like dart stuck in the awning pole above Atziri's head. "No, but then, no one has ever tried to either of us before."

Adam set his hat aside and peeked over the stern. He slumped safely below the lip of the gunwale and donned his hat again. The Yanaros were somehow maintaining their pace. But again, at least they weren't gaining. He glanced at the pistol in his hand. If it weren't for the poison darts, the *Moonflower* could just outlast them. But again, poison darts.

He holstered the Colt and turned to Atziri. "I'm going to try to speed us up, but if we can't get out of range of those darts…"

Atziri nodded. "I know."

Keeping low, Adam made his way toward the firewood, praying all the while that a dart would not find a home in his back. He reached the wood and grabbed several pieces. Opening the firebox, he tossed them in.

Water. He needed to add a bit more. He grabbed the watering can, and was thankful that it was not empty. He braced himself and got to his knees. He glanced back at the pursuing Yanaros with their headdresses of emerald green feathers. The half of the Indians not engaged with paddling, raised their blowpipes to the lips. Adam quickly unscrewed the cap on the boiler and ducked just as a trio of lethal darts sailed harmlessly over his head.

Without hesitating he rose just enough to feed water from the can into the boiler. He screwed the cap home a moment before three more dart zipped by.

He couldn't see the gauge without making himself and easy target, so he waited a few minutes for the steam to build. Then he grabbed the valve and turned it, feeding more steam into the engine.

The rhythmic puffing of the *Moonflower's* workings quickened, but if the steamer had sped up, it was not enough to notice, much less make difference.

Adam scrambled back to join Atziri by the tiller. Ahead of them the river began a wide curve to the right. Adam grabbed the map from his haversack where he also kept Father Kirby's journal. He handed the map to Atziri as he eased the wooden arm of the tiller toward himself.

He had been this far up the *Lagarto* before, but not often. "If I remember, this is where the *Blanco* joins the *Lagarto*. See which way we need to go."

Three more darts rained down on the *Moonflower*. One of the darts clinked as it bounced harmlessly off the boiler, a second overshot the steamer and disappeared over the bow. The third dart missed Atziri by a hair's breath and punched a hole through the map as she unfolded it. She screamed. Jasper squeaked and took refuge under a side bench.

"Damn, 'em!" Adam snarled. That was enough. He drew the revolver, turned to face the pursuing Yanaro and snapped off two shots. The first flew wildly off target, but the second caught the nearest Indian in the gut. The man dropped the deadly blowpipe. He clutched at his stomach as he toppled into the river.

Furious shouts rose up from the five remaining Yanaro Indians. Those with paddles redoubled their efforts to catch the *Moonflower*. The two with blowpipes loaded their darts and took aim.

13
THE MOONFLOWER BOARDED

"Adam, look out!" Atziri screamed.

Adam looked forward just in time to see the dead tree floating in the river, rushing toward them. In the moments he had spared to fire back at the Yanaros, he had neglected his hold on the tiller as the *Moonflower* entered the bend in the river.

Two poison darts whispered past on either side of him.

Even so, their pursuers would have to wait. Adam seized the long handle of the tiller and pulled hard. The *Moonflower* responded, but the tree was too close. As the steamer pulled hard to port, the branches of the tree raked the side of her hull, nearly ripping off the canoe that hung there.

The branches nudged the steamer, turning it sideways, slowing it. And it was in that moment that the first of the Yanaro dugout canoes struck her. The impact nearly sent Adam tumbling onto Atziri but he caught the nearest awning support and steadied himself.

As the first of the two Yanaro in the dugout leaped onto the *Moonflower's* bow, Adam glimpsed the other canoe just as the tree branched ensnared it and swept away down river.

Only two of the six Yanaro remained, but somehow Adam didn't feel any better about it.

The Yanrao abandoned his blowgun for an obsidian bladed dagger and he stalked toward Adam, weapon raised.

As he watched the Yanaro warrior in his war paint and shimmering green quetzel feather ornamentation inch toward him, Adam saw the river bank creeping off to his left. They were still turning back the way they had come and inching closer to the riverbank in the process. "Atziri, take the tiller! You've got to turn us around before we hit the bank!"

The Yanaro warrior glared at Atziri as she lunged for the tiller. On his dark and painted face was the same look Adam had observed when the Indians had first passed the *Moonflower*. It was a mixture of recognition and confusion.

The warrior jabbered something in a language that, had it not been for the fierceness in his tone, might have sounded almost birdsong. Atziri, who was still leaning into the tiller stared at the man with an astounded look upon her beautiful face.

Then the warrior's gaze shot fleetingly toward the river. Adam chanced a look in the same direction and saw that his companion in remaining dugout canoe was closing in on the *Moonflower* once again.

Adam turned back just as the Yanaro, glinting black dagger outstretched, lunged at him for a quick kill. Adam whipped the old Colt revolver up and fired. He almost missed entirely, but the warrior shrieked as the bullet plowed a furrow across the flesh of the man's bare rib cage.

In his surprise, the Yanaro dropped the dagger. He looked up from his wound, his face met with the back of Adam's hand. The blow sent the Indian toppling over the gunwale and into the river with a splash.

Atziri was still leaning on the tiller arm and now, the *Moonflower* was arcing back around the dugout canoe. The Yanaro paddler was too preoccupied with pulling his wounded companion into their canoe to focus on the steamer.

The *Moonflower* continued circling out into the river, to once again head upstream. Adam stood and watched the Yanaros. He raised his pistol and sent a bullet through the bottom of the wooden canoe.

"That should slow them down," he said to Atziri. He sat down next to her and took the tiller.

As the *Moonflower* headed upriver once again, Atziri turned back and watched the two Indians as the swam to shore. "Did you see how they looked at me?" she asked. "It was as if they recognized me."

Adam felt a bit hesitant. "Well, you've lived in Mar Azul since you were a toddler. They couldn't have recognized you. It had to be your tattoo."

"I suppose so," Atziri conceded. "But they definitely came after us because of me." She looked at Adam with worry in her eyes. "You had to shoot one of them because of me."

Adam felt his heart swell. He placed an arm around Atziri. "I didn't shoot anyone because of you. I shot him because they were trying to kill us with poison darts. That was their choice, Atziri. A bad choice, but their choice nonetheless."

For a moment, Atziri stared quietly at the Yanaro warriors dwindling in the distance behind them. Finally she turned to face forward and laid her head on Adam's shoulder. "You're right, my love. I guess the question now is what were they doing this far down river?"

Adam reached over and pulled his haversack close. From it, he took the journal disguised as a Bible. "If I had to guess, I'd say they were after this."

Atziri took the thick book and flipped through the pages. "Father Kirby's journal. Then it must definitely lead the way to the *Kingdom of the Jaguar People*."

Adam agreed. "They must have known that Chano Villatoro had it and they killed him in trying to get it."

Atziri snapped the journal shut and handed it back to Adam. "Then we should stay vigilant in case there are more Yanaro between here and wherever the journal is leading us."

Something clanked in the bow. Instantly on edge, they looked forward just as Jasper's tiny head popped up from among the boxes of their stowed provisions.

Atziri laughed as the Capuchin monkey extracted himself from the supplies and came capering toward the safety of Atziri's lap.

Adam laughed too.

The *Moonflower* steamed upriver, carrying them ever closer to whatever mysteries awaited them in the remote heart of the Nicaduran jungle.

14
ABDUCTION

Four days and five tributaries after leaving Mar Azul, Adam and Atziri had traveled as far as possible in the *Moonflower*. The water had finally become too shallow for the steamer. Any further progress by water would be in the canoe they had brought with them. And even that, according to the map and the journal would only take them so far toward their goal; the darkly fabled *Kingdom of the Jaguar People*, home of the savage, purportedly cannibalistic Yanaro Indians, where they hoped to find some clue to the fate of Father Kirby and the crew of *la Tortuga,* who had all gone missing seeking the *Treasure of the Jaguar King*.

Following the attack while cruising up the *Rio Lagarto*, there had been no further encounters with the very real, very hostile, Yanaro warriors. Even so, neither Adam or Atziri believed that they had seen the last of them.

The waning day was lethargic, the insects buzzed, and the rain was constant. Adam, Atziri and Jasper, sat under the awning of the anchored *Moonflower* and picked at their lunch of canned and dried foods. The oiled canvas did an admirable job of keeping the rain out; allowing only the random droplet to slip through.

"You think *la Tortuga,* made it further upriver?" Atziri asked as she handed Jasper a tin cup full of fruit. The monkey chirped excitedly and scampered off with his prize.

"That's my guess. They would have passed through here near the end of the wet season; the river might have run a bit deeper at that time."

Regardless, *the Moonflower* had come as far as she could.

Adam set the journal aside and took up the map. "Arziri, we'll take the canoe as far as we can but, after that..." He wondered if Atziri had really, truly considered trekking through the untamed, and essentially uncharted jungle. It was one thing to travel by boat, or even canoe, but eventually they would have to hack and slash their way through the densest jungle in all of Nicaduras. "I mean, if we're going to change our minds, this is the time."

The young Indian woman looked insulted and Adam immediately regretted having opened his mouth. "You mean turn back?" she said. "You think I am not up to the task?" She stood up, hands on her hips. Her copper complexion darkened in tandem with her mood. "How dare you think such a thing. Father Kirby means as much to me as he does to you. And more than that, more than that, there is this!" She touched her fingers to the tattoo along her hairline.

"Atziri," Adam said placatingly, "I know you've always hoped to learn where you came from, who your people are but, is it really so important as to justify the risk?"

Atziri scowled down at him in cold, unforgiving silence.

Adam squirmed uncomfortably.

"Yes, I do," Atziri said at length.

Adam sighed. "Alright, then, I suggest we pack everything we might need and then get some sleep. Tomorrow will be the first in a series of big days."

Darkness fell quickly in the perpetual gloom beneath the jungle's multi-tiered foliage. By the time they had their haversacks and all the provisions they thought they could carry ready and had secured the mosquito netting, the lantern offered the only light by which to see.

They settled down and, as had become their custom, lay silent and vigilant, listening to the cacophonous sounds of the jungle.

After several minutes, Adam rolled over and kissed Atziri. "Sorry," he said.

She kissed him back. "I know."

Adam could see the playful smile on her face before she closed the lantern's valve and amber glow slowly dimmed to black.

****

Adam felt Atziri slide her arm across his chest. His eyes fluttered open just enough to glimpse the first rays of sunlight reaching down through the understory. He yawned and closed his eyes, unwilling to spoil the moment. Prior to this trek into the jungle he and Arziri had never even slept in the same room, much less together.

He smiled contentedly. His thoughts, as gauzy as the steamy mists he knew to be rising from the jungle floor. He thought of Father Kirby and the others, of the Yanaro. But mostly, he thought of the future, of captaining the *Moonflower* up and down the *Rio Lagarto* with Atziri, by then his wife, at his side.

As his thoughts drifted, he felt the weight of Atziri's arm on his chest increase, a lot. He realized then he the weight wasn't just confined to his chest. He could feel it up and down the length of his body. He opened his eyes again and looked.

"Ah!" He tried to sit upright, but a green anaconda had piled itself on top of him. "Atziri," he hissed so as not to startle the massive snake.

Atziri did not reply. His heart quickened for fear that the anaconda had gotten her.

The snake's head swung toward his face and Adam quickly, but cautiously seized the serpent by it's neck near the base of it's skull. The anaconda's mouth opened wide, revealing its fangs and long flickering tongue. It hissed angrily and the coils of its long body began to writhe as it sought to wrap itself around Adam.

Adam pushed the head aside and extracted himself from beneath the snake. He stood quickly and shoved the anaconda aside. He leaped toward the *Moonflower's* cool boiler, positioning the bulk of it between him and the snake. Instead of attacking, the snake slithered over the gunwale and into the shallow water.

Adam looked around desperately. Where was Atziri? Where was Jasper? They couldn't have wandered off, wouldn't have. He did a quick inventory. Nothing, including his haversack, which he had used as a pillow, seemed disturbed or missing. He opened the sack and was relieved to find the journal, the map, and even his revolver and ammunition safely inside. Only Atziri and Japser were unaccounted for.

He drew the revolver and made sure the cylinder was loaded.

Stay, calm, he urged himself. *Atziri, is probably just be out relieving herself.* He looked around but saw no sign of her, or even their monkey.

Pistol in hand, he stepped from the anchored steamer onto the leaf strewn riverbank. Almost at once, he saw the footprints. Booted footprints. They were almost certainly not made by Indians, Yanaro or otherwise.

Suddenly, something came crashing through the jungle on his left!

15
THE VEIL OF HEAVEN

Adam spun just as the thing burst from the greenery. It happened so fast that he never even raised his pistol to shoot, and luckily so. The familiar form of, Jasper, latched onto his chest and scrambled up to his shoulders. The frantic monkey chirped and squealed. Adam had never seen him so agitated before.

"Easy, Jasper. Easy, buddy."

After a bit, the monkey calmed down, though he was to remain fidgety for some while.

Adam stood and regarded the jungle in silence for several moments. Finally, he convinced himself that Jasper had not been pursued. "I guess your telling me what happened and where Atziri is now, is probably too much to hope for, isn't it?"

The monkey made no response, his little brown eyes darting from the jungle, to the boat, to the river, and back again.

Adam holstered the Colt and returned his attention to the booted footprints that he had found in the soft earth of the river bank. The impressions were much deeper than his own, as though the owner of the boots had been encumbered by extra weight.

Atziri.

With Jasper upon his shoulders, Adam followed the footprints a dozen yards up the river. In the muck of the shallows, as saw drag marks left by a dugout or some other small boat.

"Is this the way they took, Atziri?" he asked the monkey though his gaze never left the river. Adam felt a cold resolve settle in his chest. He had no idea how much of a head start Atziri's abductors had on him but, he vowed to himself, he would catch them. He turned on his heel and headed back to the *Moonflower*.

The canoe they had brought with them still hung on the side of the steamboat. He untied the ropes that held it fast and set the slim craft on the riverbank.

He wondered why it hadn't been scuttled. For that matter, why hadn't *he* been scuttled. It seemed logical enough to him that he still had the journal and his firearm only because he had used the haversack in which he stored them for a pillow.

But, on the whole, he could only assume that whoever had taken Atziri had not wanted to risk confrontation, or perhaps, Atziri had intervened. Whatever the reason, they had made a mistake that that they were going to regret.

****

In spite of the urge to hurry, Adam paced himself as he paddled the canoe upriver. The tributary was rather narrow, just wide enough to create the random gaps in the green world above. He paddled in silence, ears and eyes vigilant for threats that could come from either bank. Vigilant, even though he knew that a poisoned dart could strike, and its toxin kill him before he even sensed anything was amiss.

Jasper roamed the confines of the canoe, climbing repeatedly over the boxed provisions and the rolled bedding that Adam had brought with them. At times, the Capuchin sat in the bow, at other times, he sat clinging to Adam's leg. It was a repetitious pattern that lasted for ours.

Around noon, Adam found a tree extending low out over the water. He tied the canoe to one of its limbs and settled down for a quick bite to eat and a review of the map and journal to get his bearings.

He hated beans, but unless he felt like spending time hunting, time he did not have, beans it had to be. He handed Jasper a bit of dried fruit and they began to eat as Adam unfolded the map. He traced his finger along the route traveled thus far. He tapped the map. "Here we are, Japser."

Still holding the half eaten fruit in one hand, the monkey leaned overly close, like a farsighted child, and regarded the map where Adam was pointing. He looked up at Adam almost quizzically. Then with a satisfied squeak, he turned his attention back to his meal, leaving a tiny, wet hand print on the map.

Adam set the can of half eaten beans aside. He had had all he could stomach. He looked further upriver on the map. There was a waterfall, next to which Father Kirby had written, *Cascada Velo del Cielo.* "The Veil of Heaven waterfall." He kept reading. *From here we shall go afoot... if, I survive the climb, that is.*

Adam sighed and picked up the beans. "Sounds like I'm going to need the energy," he said to a Jasper.

When he was finished, he rinsed the empty can and stuffed it under his seat. As he was gathering up the map and the journal, one of the many folded papers fell out. It was the portrait that Ed Matthis had drawn of Atziri before leaving Mar Azul aboard *la Tortuga.*

It looked so much like a photograph. Adam stared into the familiar coal-black eyes, shaded beneath lashes as lush as the jungle that had spawned Atziri's people. He felt a welling of desperation in his heart. If she was harmed or injured in any way...

****

Adam heard the *Cascada Velo del Cielo* long before it came into view. At first it had been like a wind rustling the leaves; a wind that grew in strength until it became a ceaseless roar.

Adam paddled the canoe around a bend and came to the head of the river: the point where it flowed forth from an ethereal, misty mountain lake. It was the first wide open sky he had seen in days and it was a sight to behold. To the left and right, the emerald shorelines stretched out and away, only to curve inward again until both shorelines came together, fading into a massive cloud of mist at the base of the towering, craggy waterfall.

Velo del Cielo. The Veil of Heaven.

Adam raised his binoculars. The river that fed the falls had, over the ages, cut a notch in the rocky face of a cliff that gave no indication of terminating in either direction. Adam sighed. "I guess Father Kirby was right, Jasper. We have tough climb ahead of us."

He trained the binoculars on the waterfall itself. Those who came before him had surely left their canoes behind. He would put in at the same point to seek a way up. Sure enough, he saw two canoes, and at least one dugout canoe half hidden in the undergrowth to the right of the waterfall.

Adam then panned the binoculars over the cliff face, hoping to see the way up. The black rocks, covered with moss and ferns, looked wet and slippery. A treacherous climb at best, he thought. There appeared to be a ledge or two, good place to rest if necessary.

He was just about to lower the binoculars and take up his paddle when a flash of blue and white movement caught his eye. He focused on the rocky outcrop and his heart leapt. Atziri!

He strained to see more detail, but the distance was too great, and the gauzy veil of mist too obscuring. She seemed unharmed, but she was not alone. Adam could not make out the other person, next to Atziri, but it was clearly a man; dressed in what, from this distance appeared to be light khaki clothing. Her captor. And from what he could tell, the man was directing her upward, but Atziri was resisting. Adam tossed the binoculars aside and began to paddle.

He had to reach, Atziri!

16

THE FALLS

Adam rowed furiously toward the abandoned watercraft at the base of the falls, eyes on the black, craggy cliff face, until the angle and the mists conspired to hide Atziri and her captor from his view. He skirted the roiling cloud of mist created by the plunging water and rowed until the hull of his canoe grated up on the stony shore.

Getting out, he pulled the canoe clear of the waterline. Jasper hopped from the boat and onto a nearby boulder, water-slick and moss covered.

Adam grabbed his haversack then looked up at the wall of water to his left. In spite of his urge to hurry, took a knife from his haversack and cut a length of oiled canvas from their spare tent. After that, it took but moments to wrap and bind the journal and its contents, including the map and portrait of Atziri in a few extra layers of protection against the water.

Satisfied that he had everything he needed, or at least as much as he could carry, he started forward. He hoped that Atziri's resistance was enough to buy him some time.

As Adam began to climb, Jasper took off, bounding upward from rock to rock, tree limb to tree limb. "Jasper! No, come back!" Adam cursed vainly against the roar of the falls. The last thing he needed was for Jasper to telegraph his presence.

He climbed faster up the slick rock face, finding purchase when he could on fern and moss and root. He reached for a small outcropping of rock only to have it shatter before he could lay his hand upon it. He never even heard the shot. He glanced up and found himself staring into Ed Matthis' snarling face.

Ten feet of treacherous stone and mist swirled air, separated Adam

The artist yelled something. Then realizing that Adam could not hear, Matthis drew Atziri into view, turning the pistol toward her as he did so.

If Atziri was worried, it did not show. For as soon as she saw Adam, her face lit up with a confident smile. A smile that wilted as Matthis trained his pistol on Adam once again.

Adam clung frozen to the rocks, waiting for some opportunity to draw his own revolver and take a shot at Matthis. Atziri said something; lunged for Matthis' weapon. The artist shoved her back from the ledge, out of sight and fired at Adam.

The bullet struck his forearm and he lost his hold. As he tumbled backward into the waterfall, he caught glimpse of Atziri as she leaned over the cliff. Adam saw her silent scream as Matthis held her back.

The next moment, the world was a roaring gray rush as the torrent drove him down like a hammer. The air rushed from Adam's lungs in a single, powerful blast as he hit the churning water of the lake. He was swirled and buffeted, breathless and disoriented.

Then, as though being regurgitated by the very waters that had tried to consume him, he found himself on a solid, if wet foundation. Adam gasped and coughed, spitting water, as he heaved himself onto his hands and knees. He found himself in a cavern, illuminated by a pale, wavering light; light that radiated through the waterfall at his back.

Even his before eyes adjusted he knew that the floor was unnaturally level, could feel the tightly fitted flagstones it was composed of.

His haversack was wet of course, but it had kept most of the water out. He found that the oiled canvas, with which he had wrapped his possessions, had done a splendid job keeping things acceptably dry. He switched on his flashlight and almost fell backward into the pool. Before him loomed a life-size stelae of a jaguar in human form. In each fore paw it held a carved human limb, one leg, and one arm ; a frightful warning to anyone who might enter this dark and unexpected place as he had.

Adam felt something on his back and was amazed to find that his hat, still hanging by it strap, had somehow survived the watery gauntlet.

His initial surprise behind him, Adam panned the light around the chamber. That it was a natural cavern was now evident by its jagged and irregular nature. But it had been greatly modified by ancient craftsmen. Their handiwork abounded in an assortment of unsettling statues and wall carvings, as well the floor, and to his relief, a flight of steps carved into the back of the chamber.

He was about to hurry up the stairs when something glinted in the beam of his flashlight. In a wall niche, upon the neck of a two foot tall, half-man, half-jaguar statue, hung a pendant; a golden disk like a calendar stone, with an emerald eyed jaguar and ruby eyed spider circling the center, locked in a mutual chase.

Adam wasn't superstitious by nature, but something stayed his hand, some sense of foreboding hung about the ornament. But then, *it's just jewelry*, he said to himself. Something Atziri might like to have when this was all behind them.

He took the necklace and deposited it into the pocket of his trousers.

Then he turned and hurried up the steep, winding stairs.

****

Eventually, the narrow stairwell began to brighten from somewhere above. Winded and legs aching from the climb, Adam switched off his light to conserve the battery and returned it to his haversack.

He came to a carved, rectangular portal that was choked nearly shut by broad leaves, vines, and roots like prison bars. He crept to the opening. The sound of the waterfall was muted to the point that he could hear the squawks of birds and the hoots of monkeys.

He thought of Jasper then. He hadn't seen the faithful Capuchin since the monkey had raced ahead of him to get to Atziri. If Matthis hurt, Jasper...

He drew his revolver and slowly pushed his way through the wall of greenery.

17
RUN THROUGH THE JUNGLE

The doorway, carved into the living rock where the river poured over the cliff and into the lake below, opened onto a beautiful glade. In the center of the clearing, brooded a colossal stone head at least three yards tall. Like the Olmec heads far, far to the north, the head was adorned with a craved war helmet. But this was no Olmec head, it lacked the round and stately features. This face was a hideous sight. While human in most respects, there were two notable exceptions. Like the stylized jaguar carvings, or even a Quetzalcoatl, the feathered serpent of the Aztecs, the mouth was home to a collection of blunt, over-sized fangs.

From between the fangs, extended a huge tongue covered in dark stains. It took but a moment for Adam to recognize the stains for what they were; dried blood. The massive tongue was clearly a sacrificial altar.

Yet more striking than the fangs and the altar, was what appeared to be four sets of sinister eyes.

The angry, stone eyes seemed to glower at Adam as if, by stepping forth, he was defiling this place of sacrifice.

As he stared at the stone head, he thought of the pendant in his pocket, that he'd taken from the cavern below the falls. It seemed to call out to him and, for a moment, Adam felt a compulsion to return the ornament to where he had found it. But only for a moment.

He looked away from the giant head. *It's just a rock. A big, damned ugly rock, but just a rock.* Even so, in spite of the heat and humidity, Adam felt a chill settle over him. He tightened his grip on the butt of his revolver, aware that his palm was soaked in cold sweat.

Heart thumping loudly in his own ears, Adam scoured the scene for some sign of Atziri and Matthis. He saw nothing, not even an indication of the direction they had gone.

His pounding heart jumped at the sound of something moving above and behind him, in the foliage that grew from the rock face in which the doorway had been fashioned. He swung the pistol around as he turned and fired. The bullet narrowly missed the furry, black and white object dropping toward him.

"Jasper?!"

Adam caught the Capuchin monkey with his free hand and raised him to his shoulder. "Jasper, all I can say is, you must have a guardian angel looking after you. You almost got shot. You really, I mean really, have to stop jumping out at me like that. I..."

"Adammmm!"

"Atziri!" *She must have heard the gun shot. She knows I survived the fall*, he reasoned.

"Jasper, old man, what do you say we go rescue, Atziri?"

The monkey squeaked and looked to the jungle in the direction Atziri's voice had come from.

****

Matthis was making no effort to flee quietly. The constant crash of his flight through the undergrowth was unmistakable. And with Atziri as his hostage, the artist was not moving quickly to escape.

Adam knew that he was gaining, that he would catch up to them was just a matter of time. Unless - and it was the only reason he could think for Matthis' recklessness – the man had a boat of some sort. Should he reach that boat in time, Adam would be hard pressed to catch them.

Adam leaped onto a fallen tree and bounded well away from where it lay, mindful of the threat of snakes. To his left, between him and the unseen river, Jasper was swinging from tree limb to tree limb.

"Don't get ahead of me this time, you hear me Jasper?"

The Capuchin monkey swung across his path but kept relatively close to Adam.

Two gunshots cracked the air! Adam dropped to the ground and scrambled to the trunk of a wide tree. Jasper dropped down beside him.

"That's far enough, Mr. Conrad!" Matthis called out.

Back against the tree trunk, Adam drew his revolver and listened. There was no sound of movement, but he could hear the hushed flow river. There had to be boat and Matthis was intent to board it without interference.

Jasper became restless, began to squirm, his tiny eyes darting this way and that among the greenery.

"Easy, little guy," Adam whispered. "I won't let him hurt, Atziri."

He set his hat aside, and slowly leaned to his right to peer around the river side of the tree. He could see neither Matthis or Atziri, but through a gap in the trees, he could see the river. He could also see the end of a canoe, which meant that Matthis was still nearby, just waiting his chance, biding his time for Adam to make a careless move. Adam hated chess.

Jasper let out a sharp screech. Startled, Adam turned back, almost into the path of the poison dart! The lethal projectile stuck into the tree, next to his head.

He could barely believe his eyes. There, not twenty feet behind him, stood two Yanaro Indians. And not just any two, but the same pair he had left flailing in the *Rio Lagarto*, near Mar Azul. He knew, because one of them wore a poultice over the injury to the side of his chest where Adam had grazed him with a bullet.

"Time to go, Jasper!"

As he lurched to his feet, Adam heard the sharp, short blast of air as one of the Yanaro launched another dart from his blowgun. The needle-like missile zipped by, vanished into the foliage. Adam rounded the tree, putting it between him and the Yanaro, at least for the moment.

Matthis yelled from the concealment of the denser jungle ahead. "You're a fool, Mr. Conrad!" And then he sent another bullet in Adam's direction.

Two poison darts whistled past.

Adam plowed through undergrowth, keeping to the trees as much as possible.

Matthis fired again. A low limb of the tree nearest Adam exploded as the bullet tore through it.

Again, through breaks in the trees, Adam glimpsed the river. He turned hard in that direction and barreled ahead. A moment later, be burst from the tangled forest, stepping out into the open air. Jasper screeched and leaped from his shoulders, and disappeared into the leaves overhanging the river.

Adam landed on a wide, sandy bank, his legs folded under him. He had dropped his revolver as he fell and he saw it now, on the damp sand, several feet away.

Before he could right himself, he saw the Yanaros drop to the sandy expanse like two jaguars, a few yards to his left.

Still on his knees, Adam turned to face them, trying not to let his eyes betray the location of the pistol.

Suddenly. They Indians looked past him in surprise.

Matthis, dragging Atziri through the sand and water with him, approached on his right. "Well I didn't expect them," the artist quipped.

The Yanaro, seeing Atziri, dropped to their knees, but they never completely let Matthis or Adam out of their sight.

"Atziri, are you hurt?" Adam asked.

The Yanaro began to jabber amongst themselves.

"What are they saying?" Matthis snarled at Atziri.

"How do I know?"

He grabbed her hair and twisted her head to look her in the eye. Adam tensed, but Matthis quickly trained his pistol on him "Don't lie to me, girl. They're your people."

"They aren't my people."

Matthis sneered. "They seem to think so. And that lovely tattoo of yours certainly says so."

As though reacting to Matthis' treatment of Atziri, the Yanaro sprang into action. Drawing their chert daggers, they darted one to the left, toward the flowing waters, and one to the right toward the steep river bank and the jungle.

Matthis took aim at the Yanaro circling toward him on the river side, fired and missed.

In that same moment, Adam dove for his own firearm.

18

THE VOLCANO STIRS

As the Yanaro closed in on Matthis from either side, the artist headed for a small, slender boat partially visible, several yards behind him. He forced Atziri along with him. She struggled and fought, but Matthis was twice her size. Matthis fired and the Yanaro stalking him from the tree line.

Adam didn't wait to see if the artist had hit his target. He snatched up his own pistol and aimed for Matthis. He cursed, realizing that the risk to Atziri was too great.

The sound of thunder broke over the river fight, giving everyone pause to turn their eyes to the strikingly clear blue sky above the watercourse. A heartbeat later, the earth trembled, bringing the fight to a standstill.

The Yanaro warrior in the shallows pointed west, up the length of the river. Adam looked and gasped. Between the trees on either bank, the nearby mist shrouded mountains were visible. The foremost of which was billowing smoke like a black cloud factory.

A volcano.

The limbs of the leafy jungle giants began to shake, their rustling leaves sounding like a rushing wind. Dead and dying branches began to fall to earth.

The river became agitated and choppy.

Then the rumbling of the volcano began to subside.

And the Yanaro, as they had upon seeing Atziri close up the first time, dropped to their knees like supplicants, chanting in their strange, bird-like language, as if no one around them existed, much less posed a threat.

Adam might have wondered at their behavior had a new sound intruded upon the scene. He looked, only to find that Matthis was getting away in the small boat - a boat propelled by a small motor – and Atziri was with him.

With the last rumblings of the volcano ringing in his ears, Adam glanced back at the still prostrate, still chanting, Indians. If he was going, now was his chance. Keeping a watch on the Yanaro, he slowly, eased back toward a cleft in the undercut riverbank. Then he turned and bolted into the jungle.

****

As Adam slipped into the greenery, running parallel to the river, and Jasper came swinging down, leaping from branch to branch.

"No time for surprises, eh, Jasper?"

The volcano had fallen silent, as though it had never rattled the heavens or shaken the earth.

Every so often, Adam slowed to listen for the boat motor. He also kept a watch on his back trail for any sign of the Yanaro warriors. But like the volcano's fury, both Matthis and Atziri, as well as the Indians seemed to have been swallowed by the jungle.

Adam consulted the map. Jasper squatted beside him as though he too was studying the drawing by Father Kirby. Thinking of the beloved old priest and what his present situation might be, Adam couldn't suppress a growing sense of dread; a sense that Father Kirby was no longer among the living. If the jungle hadn't claimed him, the Yanaro might well have and, if the Jaguar People had not authored his end, the treachery of Ed Matthis almost certainly had. Things did not bode well for the old priest or any of the crew of *la Tortuga*.

Adam pushed such thoughts from his mind and concentrated on the map. He found the waterfall, and next to the tiny sketch marking the location, Father Kirby had written the words, "Spider People". Adam thought back to the bizarre stone head with its eight eyes and other freakish features and shuddered; all the more for the fact that the sacrificial stone altar had not appeared neglected.

From there, Adam soon determined his location with a reasonable level of confidence. Not far ahead, there were drawn several mountains, but nothing on the map indicated a volcano among them.

The river alongside which he was traveling, ended at the base of one of the mountains. He glanced out over the river again. Unless he was mistaken, the mountain in question was the volcano.

On the map, a short line led from the mountain to the last notation on the map. The writing had been smudged. The sun shone over the river. Adam lifted the map up, so that the sun radiated through the old, yellowed paper. Just as he had hoped, he could just tease out the writing.

Adam's eyes grew wide and he read the words aloud. "Herein lies the Kingdom of the Jaguar King and his fabulous treasure. Woe unto those who seek it."

Adam could not help but to think of his parents, of Father Kirby, of Captain Fenton and the crew of *la Tortuga*. In the end, they had all sought the treasure, whatever it was, and in the end, they had all vanished in the attempt.

Atziri. Adam want resolution, one way or the other concerning his family and friends, but more than anything now, he wanted Atziri back.

He folded the map, tucked it into the journal, then wrapped them both in the oiled canvas and returned them to his haversack.

He stared up at the sleeping volcano, convinced that it was his destination; that it held the answers to his life's greatest mysteries.

He might not be able to catch up to the boat carrying Matthis and Atziri, but so long as he could stay one step ahead of the Yanaro warriors, he would get there. He suffered no doubts about it.

19
CITY OF THE JAGUAR KING

There was no further rumbling from the volcano that day or the next. Nor was there any sign of continued pursuit by the Yanaros. It seemed that they had faded away like the morning mists, or a bad dream. Still, Adam couldn't shake the feeling that trouble was closing in on him from all sides.

Following the river, he and Jasper had a relatively constant view of the volcano. Although quiet and still now, the mountain issued a steady plume of steam. At night, when Adam sought refuge in the branches of the trees, the unseen glowing heart of the volcano illuminated the plume with a hellish orange glow.

After two days the mountain seemed no closer than when he'd first beheld it, but on the third day, the illusion was to be broken. The way had been growing steadily steeper, taxing Adam's already weary muscles, when he entered the valley from which the river issued.

The valley narrowed, the river thinned, and the canopy of the trees thickened to the point where the waterway coursed through a vaulting tunnel of green. Shielded from the noonday sun, the forest floor was oppressed by deep, foreboding gloom.

Jasper, who had been bounding about the understory, swung down to ride on Adam's shoulder.

At length, the valley constricted until it became a deep, verdant gorge, with trees and other plants clinging to its steep and craggy sides.

Adam paused at the mouth of the gorge. On the lush bank, half hidden among the broad-leafed undergrowth, he found Matthis' small boat. He looked inside and was thankful to find no blood, no sign of struggle. In the mud, he found two pair footprints, one large, one small.

The tracks appeared fresh, from sometime today to be sure. Either Matthis was confident in his lead, or Atziri was hampering their progress. Whichever the case might be, Adam's spirits were boosted, knowing that he was on the right trail and gaining.

Adam looked to the entrance to the gorge. He could hear the rush of water, amplified by the high walls as the river issued from it, but he could see nothing in the Stygian darkness where it seemed the sun never shown. He fished his flashlight from his haversack.

"Let's hope the battery lasts," he said to Jasper.

The Capuchin monkey chittered nervously.

Adam turned the light on and entered the gorge.

The blackness swallowed him up. Spiderwebs clung to him in great sticky masses as he pushed his way through them. Things unseen hissed at him, while other things slithered and skittered at the periphery of the flashlight's beam.

It felt like hours but, according to his wristwatch, he emerged from the gorge after only thirty minutes. He looked up and the mountain was all he could see.

Adam swore under his breath. For whatever reason, when preparing to undertake this journey, he had not anticipated all of the damnable climbing. Of course, it wouldn't have mattered if he had. There was no place from Mar Azul to Cabo de Sol where he could have acquired climbing equipment had he wanted to.

He considered resting a bit before beginning his assault on the mountain but he thought of the Yanaro warriors somewhere behind him. He hoped that they had given up the chase, but he knew better.

He spent a few minutes pacing before the mountain before finding what appeared to be the most accessible point of ascent. There was no indication – no footprints, no trampled plants, no broken or cut branches – that Matthis and Atziri had climbed up this same way.

He thought of Atziri and felt a pang in his chest. She was adventurous in her own way, but Matthis was driving her hard, the thought made Adam's blood simmer in his veins.

Thinking of Matthis and Atziri, reminded Adam of the sketch the scoundrel had made of Atziri. And in turn, he thought of Father Kirby's journal, disguised as a Bible.

Chano Villatoro had died, dressed as a Yanaro, in possession that journal. The question was had he died to possess it, or had he died to deliver it?

Adam took the cloth wrapped book from his haversack and held it in his hands. He wished now that he had had time enough to read it. But, with the miserable light by which to read, the non-stop rush through the jungle, and the subsequent exhaustion, he had done little more than leaf through its cluttered pages from time to time.

Something told him that the journal was key to whatever lay ahead. That being the case, Matthis would no doubt want the journal. Why the man hadn't taken it when he had kidnapped Atziri was still a mystery to Adam. With a shrug, he returned the book to his haversack. Maybe he could trade the journal for Atziri. The question was, how to go about it? He thought about the journal and its contents and, almost at once, he struck upon an idea. Quickly, he knelt down and opened his haversack. Inside, in addition, to Father Kirby's journal, was a smaller journal in which he made nightly notes of his own progress inland. With it, was the long, slender tin containing his pen set. Adam took it out and set to work.

When he had finished, Adam repacked everything. He looked up the side of the mountain once again. He rubbed his hands together, then began to climb. "See you at the top, Jasper, old man," he said to the Capuchin.

****

When at last, Adam pulled himself up over the top of the gorge wall, he was aching, bruised, and exhausted. He rolled himself over onto his back and stared toward the heavens only to find a sky concealed behind a sunlit, though impenetrable, fog.

Jasper was waiting for him, and when he he sat up, the little monkey proceeded to rummage through his haversack for something to eat.

"Help yourself," Adam said. He looked over the edge and felt a twinge of dizziness. He scooted clear of the precipice. Concealed by the towering treetops, the jungle floor was all but invisible. Still, Adam's sense was that his Yanaro pursuers were nowhere close at hand. Or so he hoped.

Unable to find anything worth eating, Jasper abandoned his pillaging of the haversack and sat sulking in the grass next to Adam.

Adam stood then, and turned to see where he was. The mountain still towered above him, but he found himself standing upon an expansive plane. He knew at a glance that it was too level to be natural, just as he knew that the mounds that dotted it were too uniform, their arrangement too symmetrical to be the products of nature.

He lifted Jasper to his shoulder. "This was a city," he said to the monkey. "An ancient city. *The City of the Jaguar King,*" he concluded, recalling the inscription on the map. He stood a moment longer, lost in thought. *This place has been deserted for ages upon ages.* He thought of the Yanaro Indians that had been dogging his trail since just upriver from Mar Azul. If this region of the Nicaduran wilderness was their domain, one might assume they would live here. Surely they knew of its existence; knew where it was. But, he saw nothing to make him think that they, or anyone else, lived in this place.

As he considered these things, he scanned the plane for some sign of Atziri and Matthis. It was then that his gaze fell upon the pyramid. Unlike the half-crumbled structures buried beneath the voracious green of the jungle, the pyramid appeared unmolested by time or the environment. It stood near a small, mist entombed lake. The pyramid towered above everything except for the mountain that rose into the clouds behind it.

A light rain began to fall as Adam took his binoculars from the haversack and put his eyes to the eyecups. He heard Jasper screech just as something pale blurred within his field of vision. Adam felt something smash into his jaw. He staggered backward, tripped, and landed on his back, still holding the binoculars.

He stared up into the gloomy drizzle and found himself surrounded, though not by brightly plumed Yanaro warriors. The faces sneering down at him belonged to the crew of *la Tortuga*. Front and center was Captain Charles Fenton. His once jovial face, grim and agitated.

"See? I told you, boys. The lad's cut from capable cloth. I knew he'd make it. I knew he'd bring us the book."

20

BETRAYAL

Atziri stumbled out from the shadow of a towering, vine-entangled stele. Matthis, twisting her left arm behind her back, emerged on her heels. "Nobody likes a braggart, Charles."

Eyes still locked on Adam, Fenton replied. "It ain't bragging, if it's true, ain't that right, boy?"

Adam was surprised when Fenton stepped forward, and extended him a hand up. But when he reached to accept, the traitorous riverboat captain scoffed and slapped it away. "Not you, boy. Your bag. Hand it over."

Adam ignored Fenton and shifted his focus to Atziri. "Are you hurt?"

"No," she answered with a shake of her head. "You?"

"Shut up and hand over the bag!"

Adam's mind reeled at the change in Fenton. Every other year, for as long as Adam could remember, the captain of *la Tortuga* had always been a kind and jovial man. Had it been a decades long charade? A patient scheme to locate the *Treasure of the Jaguar King?* The current situation seemed proof enough that such had been the case.

Adam turned his eyes to what remained of Captain Fenton's wet and bedraggled crew. With Chano Villatoro dead, there were only two others in addition to Matthis; Simon McHenry and Cal Thompson. In the harsh light of Fenton's betrayal, Adam saw them all for the turncoats that they were. He thought of the revolver holstered on his hip. Not the best of odds, but... "Where is Father Kirby?" he demanded suddenly aware of the priest's absence.

"Oh, he's safe, don't you worry about the padre," Fenton assured him. "Now hand over the bag."

Adam slowly got to his feet. Jasper climbed quickly to perch upon his shoulder. Fenton was taller and heavier, but this was no time to be intimidated. "You didn't answer my question."

Fenton's nostrils flared. "And I gave you an order. Now, I'm going to ask it one more time. Hand it over, or I'll take it and your hand along with it." As he spoke, Fenton slipped a large knife from the back of his belt.

The rain, though light, became steady.

"We don't have time for this, Charles," said Matthis. "The savages will be getting restless soon."

Fenton's face became darker and cloudier than the agitated sky. He turned slowly to face the artist. When he spoke, his voice was low and menacing. "We've kept them at bay for weeks. Now you're suddenly afraid of stone age barbarians?"

"I'm afraid of their poison darts and arrows," Matthis said bluntly. "And now that we have this little jewel," he cupped Atziri's chin in his hand and turned her face toward Fenton. "I don't think killing another one or two of them will hold them at bay this night."

Captain Fenton gestured to Adam with his blade. "Simon, fetch me the bag," he ordered.

Simon McHenry started forward, only to stop short when Matthis said, "Careful now, our Mr. Conrad has a pistol." McHenry drew his own pistol. He pointed it at Adam and cautiously slipped the old service revolver from the holster on Adam's hip and tucked it into the front of his own belt. As McHenry reached for the haversack, Jasper hissed sharply, causing the man to flinch.

"Stupid, monkey," the man grumbled as he regained his composure. He took the haversack and tossed the bag to Fenton who glowered as he caught it but said nothing.

Captain Fenton opened the bag, looked inside, and smiled. He removed the canvas wrapped book and tossed the haversack aside. He unwrapped the journal and held it aloft for his men to see. "Never doubt me gents. The treasure is a good as ours," he boasted.

"I wouldn't be so confident," Adam said. "The last part of that journal is written in code or some weird language."

Fenton's eyes darted to Matthis then to Adam. "Bullshit."

Adam watched as the riverboat captain flipped to the last quarter of the tome; watched as Fenton brow furrowed. He had guessed right. However much Fenton had known about the journal, Father Kirby had kept some, if not all of it secret.

Fenton thumbed through the several pages of the gibberish that Adam had hastily scrawled there.

Fenton lifted his gaze from the book to to glare at Adam.

"If that's what you're looking for," Adam said. "I hope you have some way to decipher it. Otherwise its useless."

Fenton's snarl became a sly smile. "Oh, but I do," he said. He snapped the book shut and turned to the man named Thompson. "Bring the priest."

Thompson nearly tripped over McHenry in his rush to comply. Adam watched both of them disappear into the nearest ruin, only to emerge a moment later, dragging Father Kirby between them.

Adam started forward, but stopped when Fenton jabbed his pistol at him.

The old priest fell to his knees when his 'escorts' released their hold on him.

"Father!" While Adam was overjoyed that his friend and guardian was alive, he felt a bubbling anger rising within himself. The priest looked terrible. It was obvious that Fenton, or his crew, must have been roughing him up, trying to make him tell what he knew about the *Treasure of the Jaguar King*.

"Adam, you shouldn't have come," Father Kirby mumbled.

Atziri said, "We came looking for you, Father."

The priest's eyes widened at the sound of Atziri's voice. He turned his face to the ground where he knelt and shook his head. "And you definitely shouldn't have brought, Arziri."

"Enough," Fenton barked. "It's getting late and the rain is picking up." He pointed to Thompson and McHenry. "Thompson, you're on first watch. McHenry, you're in charge of the prisoners. This'll be the last night we stay on this godforsaken mountain. Tomorrow morning, we claim the treasure!"

21

DEATH BY DART

What manner of structure the ruin had been when constructed centuries ago, Adam couldn't tell. It was small, judging from the doors leading off the main room in which he and the others were gathered, consisted of four or five adjoining rooms. He imagined that it could have been the home of someone important, a noble, or a wealthy family.

The walls, although only dimly revealed by the soft amber light of their lanterns, were covered in low relief friezes depicting gods, monsters, and kings. Jaguars abounded in the imagery. Warriors, half human, half jaguar, were depicted defeating enormous spiders and even greater serpents. The spiders reminded Adam of the massive, stone altar in the likeness of human head that he had encountered above the waterfall cavern; a human head with the eyes and fangs of a spider.

He sat with Father Kirby and Atziri, who cradled Jasper in her lap, in the corner furthest from the main entrance, under the watchful glare of Simon McHenry. Nearer the entrance, Captain Fenton conferred with Matthis as the two of them studied the journal by lantern light. While somewhere out in the darkening day, the man named, Cal Thompson, stood guard against any sudden attack by the Yanaro.

"Since you have, or rather had, my journal," Father Kirby began, "I assume Chano made it back to Mar Azul. Did he come back with you? Is he out there now to help us escape?"

"He's dead," Adam said.

Father Kirby made the *Sign of the Cross*. He looked as though he had been gut punched. "How?"

Adam glanced around, then said, "He was found dead in a dugout canoe on the riverbank in Mar Azul. He was dressed as a Yanaro and I found your journal with him."

"It doesn't make any sense," Atziri said.

"Chano Villatoro, might not have had the warmest personality, but he was a just and trustworthy man. He escaped with the journal to keep it out of Fenton's hands," Father Kirby said.

Then he proceeded to explain everything.

****

"As you know by now, Adam, after your parents had vanished I had enlisted Captain Fenton and his crew to travel inland in search of answers to their fate. Cognizance of the *Treasure of the Jaguar King* was always floating in the background of our efforts. After all, how could it not be? Your parents had disappeared searching for it.

"Being considered a myth, though, it was never the *focus* of our efforts. But after two fruitless expeditions without so much as a trace of information regarding your parents, we decided to seek out the treasure in the hopes that by doing so, we might retrace their steps, and learn something of what had become of them in that way.

"I compiled every legend and story about the *Kingdom of the Jaguar People* that I could dig up. That information, along with a copy of your parents' hideous map, that I had found among their belongings in Mar Azul, became the foundation of all our subsequent efforts."

Adam shifted his gaze to Atziri's pretty face and the tattoo upon her forehead. "People used to say, Atziri was Yanaro..."

Atziri leaned closer to Father Kirby. "Am I?"

Father Kirby met her desperate eyes. "I think it is safe to say, yes. Before this expedition I doubted it. But I doubted so many things."

Atziri sat back. "Part of me always thought it was true. But the stories... if they're true too, the Yanaro are so cruel. I almost can't bear the thought."

The priest laid a hand on hers. "Atziri, my child, being Yanaro doesn't make you Yanaro. Do you understand?"

Atziri was quiet for a moment. "Yes," she said, and hugged him. "Thank you."

Father Kirby smiled and resumed his story. "Everything had gone as smoothly as one might expect on a trek so deep into the wilds, but unlike past expeditions, we knew before we began, exactly where we needed to go. It was conjecture, of course, but we had learned quite a lot over the years and I myself had made inquiries of my own between expeditions. I added these things as notes in my journal. My real mistake had been corresponding with Captain Fenton. But after all the years, I had no reason to distrust him.

"I had informed him months in advance that I was getting too old to continue these adventures but that I was willing to undertake one more. The reason, I had explained to him in my letter was that, praise the Lord, while celebrating Mass and hearing confessions in *Taam Ja'*, I had encountered an old, dying Indian with a tattoo that matched Atziri's. I showed my journal and map to the old Indian. He seemed to briefly regain some vestige of life. And speaking in a mutually understood dialect, he shared with me the information that lead here to the *Kingdom of the Jaguar People*."

Adam rubbed his chin. "But why? The Yanaro have kept themselves apart from the world for centuries. Why would the old Indian essentially draw you a map to their front door?"

Father Kirby smiled and turned to Atziri. "Because of you, Atziri. You aren't just Yanaro. You are princess. The long lost daughter of their king. It is what the tattoo represents. It is a mark of royalty."

Adam sat back against the cool stone wall and said to the priest, "That's why, when Fenton's men first brought you out of the ruin, when you saw Atziri, you said that I, 'shouldn't have brought, her here'?"

Father Kirby looked deadly serious. "The Yanaro will kill to protect the *Treasure of the Jaguar King* from us outsiders, but more than that, they will come for Atziri, and they will do whatever it takes to reclaim her."

****

Questions still bubbled in Adam's head but before he could put any of them to words, Captain Fenton loomed over their little huddle. He opened the journal to the one of the pages upon which Adam had written his imaginary code. "What does this say," he said directly to Father Kirby.

"I have no idea, Charles."

Adam winced inside. He had intended to tell Father Kirby about the purpose of the imaginary code; that it could be a means to string things along, to buy time to escape Fenton and his men. But the opportunity was gone now.

"That's what I thought," snarled the riverboat captain. "It isn't even your handwriting." He gave Adam a sour look and threw the book at him. "Nice try, boy."

Father Kirby stood up. "I told you the journal would only get us here, Charles. Locating the treasure was another matter altogether."

"It doesn't matter anymore anyway," Matthis said as he joined them. "We have the key to every lock in this godforsaken place." He gestured toward Artziri.

Captain Fenton took a cigar from his pocket. He smiled as he lit it. "That is a fact now, ain't it?"

A sudden, sharp breeze blew over them, snuffing out the match; a breeze that had blown in from behind them from one of the darkened door frames.

Adam's hand fell upon his empty holster as he spun toward the inner doorway. Something blurred past him. Father Kirby gasped as the toxic dart embedded itself in his left shoulder. He fell over, dead before he hit the floor.

22
UNDERGROUND

Adam grabbed Atziri and pulled her to the floor as Fenton, Matthis, and McHenry drew their weapons and fired several shots into the blackness. Wide-eyed, Jasper squeaked and clung to Atziri's arm.

Thompson burst into the ruin from outside, pistol in hand. "What happened? What's going on?"

Captain Fenton wheeled on him. "Get back to the front door! The damnable savages just killed the padre!"

Thompson blinked. "But how? I didn't see any..."

"There's another entrance," Matthis snapped.

"Guard that door!" Fenton bellowed as he shoved Thompson toward the main entrance.

Adam drew Atziri clear of the opening, and gave her a quick looking over as he helped her to sit up. "Are you okay?"

She was crying of course, her focus on Father Kirby's lifeless form sprawled upon the cold, ancient stone of the floor.

Adam felt a hollowness in his chest, an aching void. To lose the beloved priest now, after they had endured so much to find him...

Thunder crashed and, for a moment, Adam thought that the weather had taken a turn for the worse. The notion was quickly forgotten however, as the ground beneath them trembled. He coughed as grit and dust, shaken from the ceiling and walls fell like snow around them.

The volcano had stirred again.

There followed a commotion as Ed Thompson, the man on watch duty, rushed into the ruin. "They're coming!" he cried out.

Matthis turned to Fenton. "What do you want to do, Charles? It's getting dark. Do we make for the pyramid?"

"That's suicide!" McHenry said. "We tried that before. We'd never make it through the ruins."

As Fenton and his crew began to argue over their next course of action, Adam seized the opportunity. He whispered to Atziri. "Follow me and stay close."

Atziri blinked her tear reddened eyes and refocused herself. She nodded an cradled Jasper in her arms.

Adam slowly reached out and reclaimed his discarded haversack. "Take out the flashlight," he whispered as he handed the canvas bag to her. She looked puzzled, in a daze, but there was no time to explain anything.

McHenry stood closest to Adam. Before the crewman could react, Adam reached around and snatched his revolver from the man's waistband. At the same moment, he shoved McHenry into their group of captors.

Adam fired a shot over the heads of Fenton and the others. As they scattered, Adam grabbed Atziri by the arm and pulled her after him, through the dark door from which the poisoned dart had come.

Pistols barked, spat lead. Stone fragments flew as the bullets pinged and ricocheted off ancient walls. Adam ran blindly in the darkness, pulling Atziri with him. He slammed into the wall and chanced turning the right.

Bullets struck the wall behind them. He paused just long enough to take the flashlight from Atziri. He switched it on. The beam revealed as narrow passageway, with walls covered by faded, moss coated paintings. There was no time to spare admiring the art. The passageway descended at a steep angle. Thankfully, there was no sign of the Yanaro that had killed Father Kirby.

Behind him, he could hear Fenton and his men arguing as to who should give chase.

In the rush, Atziri had regained her composure. "Adam, where we going?"

"I have no idea," he admitted as another shot rang out somewhere behind them. "I just know we have to get away from Fenton."

"But whoever shot Father Kirby is down here."

Adam paused and shined his light back the way they had come. The beam revealed nothing in the darkness. The muffled sound of pursuit on the other hand, was clear as day. "They escaped this way, but it doesn't mean they're still here."

The flashlight beam flickered.

Atziri glanced at the light. "I suppose we'd better get moving before the battery dies."

****

The flashlight flickered with increasing regularity. From time to time, Adam slapped it against this thigh as they hurried along. The fitted stone walls of the passageway gave way to the natural irregularity of a cavern tunnel. "Why is it getting so hot," Atziri complained, as the cool, damp air became incrementally warmer and muggier.

"It has to be the volcano," Adam said, voicing the only possibility that made sense.

The flashlight flickered out and, this time, it remained so. Behind them, from somewhere up the tunnel Adam could discern at least two different voices, and they were getting closer. He felt a twist in his gut. They could not flee blindly through the blackness and they certainly could not out pace their pursuers.

Atziri clutched his shirt. "Adam, look," she whispered.

He turned in the direction that she was tugging him. He found that his eyes had adjusted to the darkness in the moments since the flashlight had died. Now he could see a faint, red-amber glow just ahead.

"It must be the way out," Atziri said. Jasper hoped from her arms to the stone floor at her feet.

The tunnel turned down and to the left, then up and left again. With every step, the glow intensified until they were bathed in a dull, orange light. Adam was wet with sweat now and he could see the beads of perspiration gathering on Atziri's face.

The tunnel opened abruptly upon a large chamber. Stalactites, glowing orange, hung thick from from the ceiling like frozen lightning. Adam looked down, expecting to see a forest of opposing stalagmites. His eyes widened. Twenty feet below, where the floor should have been, there flowed a river of steaming, slow moving lava.

A natural stone bridge spanned the molten flow.

Adam regarded the bridge with no small amount of trepidation. Where it left the ledge upon which they stood, the bridge was all of six feet wide but, further out, it was closer to two feet wide. Worse, there were places along its length where portions the bridge appeared to have crumbled away.

Adam was still pondering the stone arch, weighing their chances, when Atziri crossed her arms. "I am not crossing that," she said flatly.

Adam nodded. He wasn't feeling up to it either, but he saw no other choice. "It's either this bridge or back the way we came."

Even in the hot red light, he saw her face brighten. "Yes. Maybe we missed a turn," she said.

"That's not what I meant. I..."

The glow of lantern light began to brighten the tunnel from which they had emerged.

"Too late. We've no choice now," Adam said. He turned Atziri toward the bridge.

A tremor rolled through the cavern, loosening grit and gravel in a rain of dust. A deep basso rumbling issued from the earth like moaning giant.

"Definitely the volcano," Adam said.

The quaking was too much for Jasper. The monkey scrambled up Atziri's skirt and blouse and wrapped his arms around her neck in a needy hug.

Taking Atziri by the hand, Adam stepped out onto the bridge.

"No! I can't do it!" she implored him.

The quaking intensified and bits of stalactite began to fall from the ceiling. Adam understood then how the stone bridge had been damaged.

A bullet pinged off the mouth of the tunnel next to Adam.

"Atziri! We're dead if we stay. Now go, you can do it!"

Atziri nodded. Suppressing a sob, she stepped onto the trembling span. Adam fired a shot back up the tunnel to buy them a moment's respite, then turned and hurried after her.

Stalactites continued to fall, most of them splashing into the river of molten stone below. They were halfway across when a stalactite three or four feet long, smashed through the arch like a sledge hammer.

Atziri screamed.

23
AMBUSH

Adam grabbed the back of Arziri's huipil blouse, arresting her fall. She teetered on the edge of the newly created gap in the natural stone bridge, twenty feet above the molten death of flowing lava. The stalactite and the shattered pieces of the bridge splashed into the hot magma. Glowing red globs of melted stone flew in every direction.

Jasper leapt from Atziri's shoulders, crossed the bridge of Adam's arm, and took refuge on his shoulders.

"I've got you. I've got you," Adam said as he pulled Atziri to safety. He hugged her close.

The rumbling and shaking of the volcano subsided, and was replaced by the sound of someone clapping.

Adam looked back to the tunnel entrance. Two men stood there; one clapping his hands in a slow, steady beat, the other with a pistol trained on Atziri and himself. McHenry and Thompson.

"Looks like the end of the line, boy," McHenry called out as his hands fell silent. He drew his own sidearm and beckoned them with it. "There's nowhere to go. Now come on back, the Captain wants a word with you."

"I'll bet he does," Adam spat. He was about to say something more when Atziri, standing behind him, spoke into his ear.

"We can make it to the other side," she said.

Without looking away from Fenton's men, Adam replied. "Are you sure, Atziri? Are you absolutely sure?" He was worried that should she freeze up in the attempt, they would most certainly fall to their deaths.

He caught movement out of the corner of his eye as, without waiting, she turned and leapt over the void. McHenry and Thompson looked shocked at the unexpected turn of events.

Adam fired a shot in their direction, turned on his heel, and followed Atziri. He leapt over the missing length of stone, perhaps a yard across and landed on the downward slope of the lava carved arch.

Gun shots pinged and wanged wildly around them as Fenton's men lobbed bullets and curses.

Atziri was already on the ledge near the opening down which the tunnel continued. At first, Adam had no idea where she had found the sudden courage. Then he saw Jasper just up ahead of them. The faithful Capuchin must has crossed over before them and Atziri had followed his lead. Whatever the case might be, Adam was grateful all the same.

He caught up with them at the mouth of the tunnel.

Atziri pointed past him. "They're coming!"

As the men neared the broken apex of the bridge, Adam chanced a look toward the cavern ceiling. Sweat blurred his vision as he took aim. He wiped his eyes and fired. The bullet slammed into one one of the thicker formations, cracked it, and ricocheted into its neighbor. The second stalactite broke loose, clipped its larger companion.

McHenry looked up, eyes wide in horror. The first stalactite missed the bridge and was consumed by the lava below. The second stalactite, however, dove its ragged point though Thompson's shoulder and into his rib cage. Eyes bulging in shock, he coughed blood and toppled over.

Both Atziri and Adam turned away.

When Adam looked back, he saw McHenry back on the far ledge. The man jabbed his pistol in the air at them and yelled, "If Fenton wants your little savage bad enough, he can come get her himself. To hell with you, both!" He began to turn back up the tunnel, then paused. "You'll both likely die down here, but if I ever see you again I'll kill ya. I'll kill ya, for Thompson!" And with that he left them alone in the cavern.

****

Blackness. With the red glow of the lava chamber behind them, Adam and Atziri were soon enveloped in absolute darkness. They groped their way forward in dread of the thought of missing a passageway that might lead them out: fearful that every step would end over a precipice.

Maybe they should have chanced staying with Fenton and waiting for some opportunity to escape that didn't involve underground tunnels to oblivion. *What was I thinking, rushing down an unlit passageway after a murdering Yanaro? And dragging Atziri along with me?* Adam cursed himself.

Suddenly, the irregular surface of the tunnel wall changed. "More carvings," he whispered. "Like the entrance."

"We must be close to a way out," replied Atziri in the darkness. The tunnel rose steeply, becoming long flight of stone carved steps.

Jasper leapt to the ground and scampered up the steps ahead of them.

They emerged into the dark interior of another structure. At first, neither of them realized it. But then, a cool night breeze wafted over them. Adam turned into the wind and found himself staring out into the night through a tall, open doorway. Stars glinted.

Cautious, they crouched in the opening, listening for any sign of the Yanaro. Father Kirby's killer, if he had even come this way, seemed long gone.

"Good, Lord," Adam said. He pointed out to the night smothered plain. Beneath the half-moon, the sight of the man made tableland at night was not what he had expected. But what had he expected? an expanse of pitch black jungle scrub and overgrown ruins, one indistinguishable from the other in the darkness?

"It's... it's beautiful," Atziri murmured in amazement.

And it was.

Far across the plain, the colossal step pyramid, with the *Temple of the Jaguar King* at its peak, towered over all, illuminated by glowing threads of brilliant orange lava that trailed down the sides of the stone edifice like neatly ordered blood vessels. How the lava was channeled so, was beyond Adam. Did it flow continually or did have something to do with the stirring volcano that blotted out the starry sky behind it?

It was several moments before either of them could tear their eyes away from the distant pyramid and its orange, magmatic light. It was another light that caught their attention. To their right, and slightly behind them, down on the plain of ruins, blackness prevailed. Prevailed that was with one notable exception. A tiny cluster of yellow lights, bobbing about each other like squabbling fireflies.

Lanterns.

Fenton and his men had evidently reached the limit of their patience. That, or they were afraid to risk losing the treasure to Adam and Atziri. *Greedy bastards, Adam thought.* But what of the treasure now? He had not spent much time thinking about it, at least not in the fame and fortune sense of it.

He had thought most of Father Kirby and then, after Matthis had abducted her, Atziri. He had also wondered about the decades old mystery of his parents. But now, Father Kirby was dead, Atziri was no longer a captive and, well, was there anything he could learn about his long lost parents that would make any real difference in his life? Not really, he admitted, certainly nothing worth risking their lives over anyway.

He turned to Atziri, who seemed lost in her own thoughts. "We can turn back," he said.

"What? You mean now? Just go back to Mar Azul?"

He shrugged and explained his thinking.

Atziri placed her small hand on his unshaven cheek. "I agree. Your parents are almost certainly gone. But at least you know where you come from, who you are. I don't really know anything about who I am." With her free hand, she gestured toward the strange pyramid. "But what if my family is down there? What of they can fill in the blanks in my past? What if..."

Adam took her hand in his and gently squeezed it. Atziri wanted what he had always believed that he had wanted for himself. How could he deny her that, whatever the consequence?

"Then I guess we have a decision to make," he said.

She looked uncertain. "Yes?"

"Do we set out for the pyramid now, or wait for first light?"

Adam heard the dual puffs of air just as the thin the dart embedded itself in his shoulder.

Jasper shrieked.

The world spun. Adam saw Arziri staring at a dart protruding from her forearm. He saw the distant pyramid swirl before him in a blur of black and orange. And, for moment, the stars hung above him, then they seemed to melt away, absorbed by the infinite blackness of space.

24
THE PAST ALIVE

Kingdom of the Jaguar King
Twenty Years ago

"Come, Atziri! Hurry, child!" The old woman, naked to the waist, her skin as brown and wrinkled as and old sapote fruit peel. was painted in vibrant greens and golds. Brilliant, emerald quetzel feather depended from her ears. The only ornament she wore this dreadful day, was the family's royal pendant; A jaguar with emerald eyes pursuing a spider ruby eyes in their eternal struggle.

"I am hurrying, grandma," said the girl as the old woman half dragged her through the undergrowth.

"Then hurry more!" came the uncharacteristically harsh reply. "We must be faster than..." They burst upon a clearing and the rest of her words were drown out by the roar of a waterfall. A river ran through the glade and disappeared over the edge of a cliff. Other than the river, the clearing was dominated by a large stone taller than two men. Had it been carved, it would have made an impressive monument.

Only five years old, Atziri had never been here before; had never been this far outside of the palace grounds. She wondered where her grandmother was taking her.

"Come," the old woman said as she drew Atziri toward a particularly dense stand of trees not far from the river.

Behind them rose a chorus of shouts and war cries. Atziri glanced back one of the Ixinta, the Spider People, charged into the clearing brandishing their stone-bladed war clubs.

"We are too slow!" her grandmother cursed, but she did not stop. She pushed through the foliage, hauling Atziri along with her.

They were in a cave! Atziri realized then that her grandmother's plan must have been to hide in the cave before being seen by the Ixinta.

The cave was small, but great care had been taken to decorate it. Scenes of Yanrotequal the jaguar god and his half human, half jaguar warriors defeating the Serpent People abounded. Atziri would have liked more time to look as all the paintings, but her grandmother was already leading her down the narrow steps, deeper into the earth.

A soft roaring sound echoed up from below. *The waterfall*, Arziri surmised.

"Where are we going, grandma?" Atziri asked after several downward twists.

"You are leaving this place," the old woman wheezed.

You? Atziri did not like the way her grandmother had said the word.

"You will come too?"

Pale, flickering blue light began to show ahead of them.

"Only you, child. I will stay. I have work to do."

They reached the last steps. "But the Ixinta are coming!"

Her grand mother glanced back up the stairs, then she placed both hands on Atziri's shoulders and smiled with a gentle resolve. "The Ixinta *are* my work."

"But..."

"Hush, there is no time to argue," her grandmother said as she turned Atziri away from the steps.

Atziri gasp! Before her stood a statue. Even from behind, she recognized the powerful Warrior Jaguar god, *Chak'na'bal,* father of the Yanaro, *the Jaguar People.*

Like the real Chak'na'bal, the statue showed the god in all of his ferocious and terrifying glory; a snarling, frightful face with bulging, lidless, terrifying eyes. Most frightening of all, Chak'na'bal brandished the sundered limbs of his foes like weapons.

Atziri was thankful that Chak'na'bal favored the Yanaro People.

In seven niches in the walls of the small, misty cavern, were seven statues of the half-human, half-jaguar servants of Chak'na'bal. Although lesser deities, the Seven were often enough, all the protection the Yanaro needed.

"There," said her grandmother.

Atziri saw the small dugout canoe resting on the flagstone floor, just this side of the torrent of falling water.

"Get in. Quickly!" Atziri hesitated. "Nowwww!" hissed the old woman as the deep voice of the Ixinta warrior blasted through the cavern, louder even than the waterfall.

Atziri yelped as her grandmother shoved her into the boat and pushed it toward the wall of falling water.

Atziri sat up in the tiny, rocking canoe. Tears were streaming down her cheeks as she looked back. Chak'na'bal, fierce and powerful, glared down at her. In the stone god's shadow, Atziri watched her grandmother as the old woman moved to the statue of one of the Seven in it's dark niche.

"Grandma!"

Either the old woman could not hear her over the din of the waterfall, or she ignored her. Atziri watched as she hung her royal pendant on idol's neck.

"Grandma!"

From the shadows behind the statue, the old woman drew forth a jade bladed war club. She quickly pressed herself against Chak'na'bal, opposite the stairwell. Atziri locked eyes with her grandmother and the old woman smiled warmly.

The dugout slowly nosed into the waterfall. The force of the water striking the bow almost sent Atziri overboard. She gripped the sides of the canoe with her tiny hands for balance. The water began to press upon her back and shoulders. Like the waterfall, tears poured from Atziri's eyes as she watched the Ixinta warrior slowly approach the far side of Chak'na'bal.

Why was the warrior god just standing there? What was he waiting for? Surely he would kill the Ixinta devil. Surely, Chak'na'ba would save Grandmother.

Atziri inched toward the back of the dugout even as it carried her deeper into falling water.

"Grandma!"

It happened so fast. The serpent warrior glanced up, having apparently heard her cry of warning and in that moment, her grandmother stepped out from in front of Chak'na'bal. She swung the war club, catching the Ixinta in the stomach. The jade blades opened the man like a ripe fruit.

For an instant, Arziri was overjoyed. She would be able to go back. But in the next instant, the dying Ixinta brought his own war club down on grandmother's head. The two of them splashed into the pool and disappeared from sight.

Atziri's scream was drown out as she passed fully into the falls.

25
PIT CELL

"Wake up, boy!"

Adam's head felt as if it were packed with cotton. '*Well, at least I'm not dead*', he thought. He rubbed the tender spot on his shoulder where the toxic dart had struck him. He sat up, looked around, and instantly second guessed himself. He was dead. He was in Hell. Flickering orange torchlight, shown upon walls lined floor to ceiling with... human skulls. If this wasn't Hell, it was a runner up.

He blinked his eyes but the hellish vision remained.

"Atziri?"

"They took her somewhere else," said the voice that had awakened him.

Adam looked across the circular little chamber of skull and shadow and saw Captain Fenton sitting against the wall opposite.

"Took her where?"

"How should I know? But I don't imagine its a good thing."

Adam's head began to clear. He lurched to his feet. "Where's the door?"

Fenton gestured upward resignedly.

At least twelve feet overhead, a grated door lay across an opening. There had to be a way to reach it. He looked looked again at the wall of skulls. "What is this place?"

The older man shrugged. "End of the line?." He looked Adam dead in the eyes. "I reckon we have a better idea of what happened to your parents now."

Adam scowled. It had been all of twenty years since his parents had gone missing. He harbored no illusions that they might still be alive after all this time. "As if you ever actually cared, Captain." He turned his back on Fenton and regarded the wall of skulls. The gaping eye sockets taunted him, mocked his thoughts. How many other people had been imprisoned here, thinking they might somehow escape?

"I cared, at first," Fenton said. "But the jungle is an insatiable beast, Adam. It doesn't take long to realize as much. It consumes almost everything. And what it doesn't consume, it subsumes. Your were only human, what chance did they have?"

Adam listened, but made no reply, as he gingerly touched one of the skulls before him.

Fenton continued. "The treasure, on the other hand. Well, even the jungle couldn't claim that."

Treasure. Adam, thought of poor Atziri. He had to find her. He tested the skull in its dark mortar. It did not budge. He reached for another skull. "The jungle is probably full of lost treasure. What's so special about this one that you've pursued it for twenty odd years? You aren't getting any younger, as they say."

Captain Fenton chuckled. "The *Treasure of the Jaguar King* ain't no ordinary treasure, boy. A pair of emeralds, like the eyes of their heathen jaguar god. Have you ever heard of trapiche emeralds?"

When, Adam did not answer, Fenton answered for him. "I guess not. But then what use would a backwater river rat like yourself have for treasure, eh?" He pressed on. "A trapiche emerald has a six pointed star in it. On their own, they're rare enough. But the *Treasure of the Jaguar King* is a matching pair of fist-sized trapiches. Identical stones. *Identical.* You understand that that is all but impossible. But even more than this, they're purported to posses supernatural power."

Adam sighed and turned from his examination of the wall of skulls. "Sounds like a tall tale told by drunken men in the Anaconda, if you ask me."

Fenton shrugged. "Seems we all need something to cling to, don't we?"

Adam regarded him in silence. "If you were just after the treasure, why pretend to look for my parents for all these years."

Fenton pushed up on the short black bill of his cap, nudging it further back on his head. "No great mystery there. For one, Father Kirby, God rest his soul, could never bring himself to give up hope even in the face of ever diminishing odds. A real man of Faith he was, that one."

"And?"

"Money. Expeditions aren't cheap, you know. As long as the good Father could raise the money for the noble cause of finding your folks, the treasure hunt could continue. That, and the fact that Father Kirby kept the secrets in that journal of his as sacrosanct as the Confessional."

Adam nodded. "Would you have killed us up in the ruins, if you hadn't been interrupted?"

Fenton's brow lifted as he seemed to consider an answer. "Other men have killed for lesser things than the *Treasure of the Jaguar King*. So, to be honest, I don't know. Whose to say?"

"I don't think you would have. At least I don't think so now."

The riverboat captain chuckled. "I suppose we'll never know now, will we?"

That wasn't quite the answer Adam had hoped for, but it was good enough for now. He turned back to the wall of skulls. "I think I can use these skulls for hand and foot holds to climb up."

"Don't waste your time," Fenton said. He gestured toward a lower section of the wall next to where he sat. It was then that Adam noticed the small heap of crushed bone, crumbled mortar and a stone wall behind the macabre facade of human remains.

"It's just for looks," Fenton stated. "It won't hold any weight."

Adam cursed under his breath. He had to get out and find Atziri. "We can't just sit here."

"Why not?"

"Because of Atziri. You don't care that they have her?"

Fenton stood up. "No. Not really. You forget, she's one of them. And I'm not in the mood to risk my life for any of them. Besides..."

Adam's fist caught the riverboat captain square on the jaw. The larger man spun, his face colliding with the skulls in the wall behind him. Adam instantly regretted hitting him. Fenton might be older, but he was burly and muscular and outweighed Adam by a good thirty or forty pounds.

Captain Fenton, massaged his jaw, collected himself and turned back to Adam. "Not bad, boy. I'll give you that much. Ever try that again though, and I'll beat you to within an inch of your life."

"She's not one of them."

Fenton spat a bit of blood on the floor. "She's Yanaro and you damn well know it."

"Well... she's nothing like them and *you* know that."

Adam looked up at the grate again. They he looked at Fenton.

"What?"

"Cup your hands together like a stirrup."

"Like what?"

"Just do it."

Fenton grumbled but complied, but as Adam placed one foot in the captain's knitted fingers...

"No," Fenton stood straight. "If I try to launch you that high, I'll throw my back out."

Adam leveled a gaze at him. "You can escape with a back ache, or die in this cell in comfort. Up to you."

Fenton grumbled under his breath but cupped his hands. "Don't let me do all the work, boy."

Adam stepped into Fenton's hands and placed his own hands on the captain's shoulders. "Three. Two. One!"

Adam caught the wooden grate. He glanced down to find Fenton grinning, his back apparently just fine. Slowly, Adam pulled himself up and pressed his cheek against the grate until he could peek beyond their cell.

Something rushed at his face from the side. He gasped, lost his hold, and fell back into the cell.

26
UNDER THE WORLD

Adam crashed onto Fenton, who crumpled under the impact.

"Get off of me!" snapped the riverboat captain.

Adam glanced up at the opening for some sign of the thing that had startled him and found it staring down at him.

"Jasper?" Adam stood up. The white headed monkey chirped excitedly. "Jasper!"

"Where did he come from?" Fenton asked as he righted himself.

"It doesn't matter," Adam said, though he had to assume that the monkey had fled when he and Atziri had been ambushed and rendered unconscious.

"Jasper. Jasper, open." Adam said. As he spoke he mimed opening the grate.

"You've got to be kidding. He's a monkey."

Adam ignored Fenton. "Jasper. Green key. Give me the green key."

The Capuchin blinked then duck out of sight.

"Brilliant. Assuming he even knows what a key is, you probably just sent him off to God only knows where to look for the bloody..."

The jade pin that Adam had glimpsed through the grate bounced off the top of Fenton's cap and clattered to the floor among the skulls.

"...damned thing. I'll be damned," Fenton said as he scooped the ornately carved pin and looked up to the grate.

Adam took the pin and briefly examined it. It was a piece of milky jade, about the size of a carrot, carved in the stylized likeness of a feathered serpent. It was a treasure in its own right."

"I'll take that," Fenton snarled covetously as he snatched it away and dropped it into his pants pocket.

Adam thought of the pendant still in his own pocket and wondered what violence Fenton would resort to, to possess it, if he knew about it.

"The monkey unlocked the grate," Fenton said. "Now how do we open it?"

Adam stared up at the circular grate. "I pretty sure that I can push it aside, but you're going to have to toss me up again in order to try."

The riverboat captain huffed but cupped his hands into a stirrup. A moment, later, Adam was airborne again. His raised hand to hit the grate and it flew back on its hinge.

Before he could fall back down, Adam caught the edge of the opening. He hung there a moment, then pulled himself up just enough to survey the passageway.

Jasper was sitting patiently a few feet away. He chittered excitedly when Adam looked at him. "Good job, Jasper. Good boy."

All around the cell opening, the ruddy stone walls were lavishly painted with horrific depictions of green plumed warriors leading their conquered enemies up the steps of a great pyramid, where three priests, dressed in spider motifs, worshiping before an angry volcano, were engaged in human sacrifice.

Adam wished that he still had his revolver but, aside from the pendant in his pocket, their captors had taken everything from them. He was grateful that the Yanaro were not familiar with pockets.

He hoisted himself up and out of the cell. He looked back down at Fenton. There was no way to help him out without a rope or a ladder. "I'll be back," he said.

"What? Where the hell are you going? Get me out of here, damn you!"

"How?"

Fenton's stubbly face twisted angrily, but he said nothing. He clearly recognized his predicament.

"I'll be back, trust me," Adam assured him. Without waiting for a reply, he left the captain of *la Tortuga* in his pit cell.

He reached down, extended his hand to Jasper. He swung the monkey up to his shoulders. It occurred to him then that Jasper couldn't have just happened to find him in his cell. The trusty little monkey must have been looking for him and Atziri and, as such, must have seen much of the layout of the place.

"Jasper, where is, Atziri?" he tried.

The Capuchin hooted softly and gestured forward with a flick of his tiny wrist. Adam's hopes soared. Then he stayed himself. He wanted to rush to Atziri, but he needed help. He needed Captain Fenton.

The light in the passageway came from a single torch. He lifted it from its stone sconce and looked around. For the first time, he noticed that the passageway wasn't actually a passageway. It was a dead end, a niche, and its only prominent feature was the pit cell from which he had just escaped.

Near to the mouth of the niche he found a length of supple, fibrous rope. He plucked it from the large stone peg upon which it hung, then returned to the open pit to extract Captain Fenton.

"I found a rope," he whispered down. He quickly tied the rope to the empty torch sconce.

But just as Adam was about to drop the rope into the pit, Jasper chirped in alarm. Adam turned just in time to see a war club streaking down toward his head.

Adam hurled himself to one side. Sparked flew as the stone-edged weapon struck the floor. The Yanaro warrior never even paused. He sprang after Adam, swinging the club for a killing blow.

With no weapon of his own, Adam flung the rope at the warrior's arm, entangling it. He gave the rope a sharp pull, wrenching the warrior's arm to one side. The war club flew free. It slammed against the wall and clattered across the floor, coming to stop beyond either man's reach.

Adam got to his feet and squared off against the warrior.

"What's going on up there, Conrad!" Captain Fenton yelled. "Throw me the blasted rope already!"

"I'm a little busy right now, captain."

The warrior glared at Adam then smiled. From a scabbard on his right calf he drew wicked looking jadeite dagger.

Adam's eyes shifted toward the war club. The warrior sneered and shook his head. Adam ignored the man's confident warning and did the only thing he could do if he hoped to avoid being gutted.

He dove for the club.

The warrior dove for Adam.

"Quit horsing around!" Fenton roared. "Toss me the damned rope!"

Adam grabbed the club and raised it before himself as he rolled onto his back. The thin, rectangular blades that studded both edges of the war club were incredibly sharp. The warrior howled as the arm bearing the dagger towards Adam's heart, slammed against the stone edges

He still held the dagger but he jumped clear of Adam, clutching his bleeding arm. He seemed to hesitate as Adam stood and hefted the war club.

Not wanting to give the warrior even a moment to consider a next move, Adam charged him, swinging the club as he did.

The warrior bared a set of small, wide-spaced teeth, each embedded with a tiny emerald, and hissed furiously. With Adam giving chase, the savage warrior tuned on his bare heels and dashed toward the entrance to the niche.

He hit the outer ledge and started to turn to the right when he lost his footing. His momentum carried him out into the open air beyond. The warrior's scream trailed away as he plummeted from sight.

Adam reached the ledge and his eyes fell upon a sight he could never have before imagined. He instantly forgot about his fallen attacker.

They were underground. Deep, underground. He stood upon a ledge overlooking a cavern so massive that all of Mar Azul could have been crammed inside. A hundred feet below where he stood flowed a slow moving river of brilliant orange lava.

A rolling tremor rattled through the cavern, shaking the towering stelae, carved from the natural stone of the cave, which stood at odd intervals around the underground chamber like mighty sentinels. Adam had a sense that these rumblings, were all that uncommon in this volatile place. The walls of the cavern were lined with ledges and peppered with niches not unlike the one where he stood. Only a smattering of them were lit by torches, the rest were black as dead, empty eye sockets.

"Conrad!"

Fenton. He had almost forgotten the riverboat captain.

27
WHO'S THERE?

Torch in one hand, war club in the other, and Jasper on his shoulder, Adam crept along the ledge, past a long line of dark cell niches.

"Do you even know where you're going?" Fenton whispered sharply from behind him.

"Trust me," Adam said, though in truth he had no clue. He had told Jasper to find Atziri and, for whatever it was worth, he was taking directions from the monkey which, of course, he could never admit to Fenton.

"You're gonna get us lost."

"We need to find, Atziri."

"We need to be heading up."

"What about your men, Matthis and McHenry? You don't even care to find them?"

"They knew the risks. They're on their own as far as I'm concerned."

It was a cold sentiment. Adam knew that there was no way he could ever trust Fenton. "Then you're on your own too. Go if you want. I won't stop you," he said. "But I'm not leaving until I find, Atziri."

Fenton's thick hand clamp down on Adam's shoulder, stopping him in his tracks. "Don't try twisting my words, boy. *We* need to get out of this place. And by God..."

Jasper hissed and sank his teeth into the Fenton's hand.

"Ow! Son of a ...!" The river boat captain jerked his hand away. "The little bastard bit me!" He drew his hand back as if to strike the Capuchin monkey but checked himself when Adam hefted the war club.

"Think twice, captain."

Fenton's face darkened like a storm cloud. He opened his mouth to say something but was interrupted.

"Who is that? Who's there?"

The tension on the ledge vanished in an instant. Adam turned his attention to the darkened niche near where they stood. "Hello?"

"You speak English!" said the voice.

Adam held his torch out and cautiously and entered the niche. His first thought was that it was Matthis or McHenry, but the voice was to frail and unfamiliar. His heart sped up. Was it possible? Could it be? He was aware of Fenton behind, drawing the jadeite dagger.

He lit the blackened tip of a used torch suspended in a scone on the wall. The niche was more or less identical to the one they had escaped from. In the center of the floor was a pit cell. Adam cautiously peered down through the grate. A bony hand shielded a pair of wide, green eyes, that blinked in the torchlight. The eyes belonged to a man sitting in the bottom of the skull lined cell. He was rail thin man with long, gray streaked hair and an unkempt beard that extended down to the middle of his chest. His only clothing was dark red hip-coth belted around his thin waist.

"Father?" The word escaped Adam's lips like a desperate prayer.

The man stood up and craned his neck for a better view. "Adam?"

Adam handed the torch to Fenton. He dropped to his knees and pulled the jade lock pin from its socket, and flung the grating wide. "Go find the rope!" he ordered the captain.

A moment later, Adam lowered the rope down into the hole. The man below stepped into the looped end and held tightly as Adam and Fenton drew him up from his prison.

The man was an inch or two shorter than Adam, and looked less frail up close.

"Adam? My boy, is it really you?"

Adam wrapped the man in a hug. "Yes. Yes it's me fa..." his voice cracked. "Father."

Fenton removed his skipper's cap and scratched his balding scalp. "I'll be damned. After all these years, I can barely believe what I'm seeing with my own eyes." An excited, greedy, smile split his face. "Call me superstitious if you like, but if this little reunion is possible, then anything is... including the *Treasure of the Jaguar King*!"

Martin Conrad separated himself from his son's embrace. "Oh, the treasure is real, Mr...?"

"Fenton, Captain Charles Q. Fenton."

Martin nodded. "Captain Fenton. The treasure is as real as you or I, but if you think to escape here with it, think again."

"Who's to stop me? I've gotten this far haven't I?"

Martin waved a hand dismissively. "Only because the Ixinta are preoccupied with something."

Adam felt a chill settle over him. *Atziri,* he thought.

"Ixinta?" Fenton said. "You mean the Yanaro, the *Jaguar People.*"

"The Yanaro are no more," the elder Conrad replied gravely.

"Well then who are the savages we keep running into, these Ixinta?" Fenton demanded.

The strange spider motifs he had encounter along the way, flashed through Adam's mind. He looked at his father. "The Spider People."

"Yes," said Martin. "Centuries ago they were Yanaro. But they were branded heretics and exiled. They became known as the Ixinta. The two peoples have been warring ever since, with the Ixinta forever bent on eradicating the Yanaro and taking possession of their lands and, most especially, the treasure that empowered the Yanaro kingdom."

"I came for the treasure," Fenton insisted. "Ancient history changes nothing."

"Ancient history?" said Martin. "The Ixinta wiped out the Yanaro just twenty years ago. A near total genocide that to this day shapes their lives."

Adam looked at his father. "You said *near* total."

"A princess went unaccounted for. They have been searching for her ever since. They need her blood to awaken the *Eyes of the Jaguar* in order to make complete their conquest of the Yanaro."

Adam felt a cold fist in his stomach. "When is that supposed to happen?"

"I wouldn't worry," said Martin. "The princess has never been found so... they..." he look at Adam. "Do you know something about the princess?"

"My friend, Atziri. They have her."

Adam noticed his father's already pasty complexion pale even further. "You believe she's the princess?"

Captain Fenton snorted. "It doesn't matter if she is, or isn't. What matters is what the Ixinta believe she is."

Adam shrugged. "She has an unusual tattoo..."

"Across her forehead?" Martin asked.

For a moment, Adam thought that his father's legs were about to buckle under him.

"Then it's really happening," Martin said grimly. "This explains what the Ixinta are preoccupied with; why the there are so few of them to be seen lately."

Adam felt desperate, yet hopeful. "What do you know about what they have planned. Do you know where Atziri is?"

Martin Conrad pointed a thin finger toward the cavern's shadow shrouded ceiling. "To the *Temple of the Jaguar King*, where they mean to sacrifice her."

Adam's grip tightened on the war club. "Not if I have anything to say about it."

28
DEATH AWAITS THE UNWORTHY

There was so much Adam wanted to ask his father, so many question that *needed* asking, but they would have to wait for later. Right now, saving Atziri was all that mattered.

Adam felt Jasper's tiny hands digging into the fabric of his shirt as the little monkey clung tightly to his shoulder. He patted the Capuchin's head as Martin led them ever higher through dark and winding passages, keeping to the shadows unless their was no other choice.

"The Ixinta do not live on the plateau in the city ruins," Martin explained as they paused at the base of a stelae carved in the likeness of yet another jaguar deity. "They believe that the residual power of the Yanaro lingers there like a malevolent spirit. Only the Ixinta High Priest, Yaotyl, his two lesser priests, and their warrior-acolytes spend any significant amount of time here and that is only to keep the Yanaro gods placated."

"Heathen nonsense," Captain Fenton huffed. "If you ask me, they've just scared everyone off so they can hunt for the treasure without competition."

"They aren't hunting for the treasure, Captain. The Ixinta know exactly where it is."

Adam didn't necessarily agree with Fenton's reasoning, but what his father was saying didn't make sense. "If they know where it is, why not just take it and leave."

Martin shrugged. "From everything I've been able to gather over the years, the Yanaro are tied to the *Eyes of the Jaguar,* the *Eyes of the Jaguar* are tied to the volcano, and the volcano is the spirit of their primary Jaguar god, Yanarotequal. One cannot exit without the other."

Adam nodded. "And the Ixinta believe themselves to be the true Yanaro."

"All I know," Fenton said as they came upon a fork in the tunnel, "is that when I leave, the *Treasure of the Jaguar King* is leaving with me."

Martin paused at the fork. "You'll be lucky to leave with your life... if you leave at all, Captain."

"You've been a prisoner of the Ixinta for too long, Conrad. You've begun to believe their nonsense."

Adam glanced at the river boat captain. "Weren't you the one who said, *'What matters is what the Ixinta believe'*?"

Fenton smirked. "Touché, boy, touché"

Martin said, "Whatever you choose to believe, you're about to find out who is right. We've reached the pyramid."

Adam was instantly alert. He hefted the war club. He knew that Fenton was just as suddenly on edge.

"This is cavern system lies beneath the ruined city," Martin explained. "The right fork in leads up through the base of the great pyramid."

"Less gab, more go," Fenton urged them, his words practically dripping with lust, for the treasure.

Martin held up a cautioning hand. "Don't think that you're simply going to rush in a take the treasure, Captain Fenton. Remember, we haven't encountered any Ixinta since we started out, because most, if not all of them, are very likely in the temple atop the pyramid."

As they entered the right fork. Adam asked to his father. "Do you have any idea how many of them are we talking about?"

"There are three high priests and six or seven warrior-acolytes."

"Almost enough to make for an interesting fight," Fenton snickered.

"What, arrows and poison darts aren't interesting enough?" Adam said.

"Shhhh!" Martin pointed ahead to where the natural stone of the tunnel was replaced by massive blocks of ornately carved, carefully fitted stone. Like a giant puzzle, the carved surfaces created adjacent friezes depicting the hideous gods and frightful kings of the Yanaro-Ixinta pantheon.

Overhead, the painted ceiling was a river of stars and, shooting between them, comets with monstrous faces. Underfoot, the floor was the mirror image of the ceiling.

Thinking of Atziri, Adam was eager to continue. He stared forward when his father caught him by the arm. "Wait," cautioned the elder Conrad.

"Why? Isn't this the way?" Adam asked.

Martin nodded. "Yes, but..."

Fenton pressed close. "But what?"

"I've never been allowed beyond this point."

Fenton shrugged. "So?"

"Only the high priests are allowed. Death awaits anyone unworthy."

Adam stared as far up the passageway as the torchlight allowed. "Then why brings us this way? Why not go another away?"

"Exactly," Fenton grumbled. He looked back the way they had come, clearly suspicious of having been led into a trap.

"If the Ixinta intend to sacrifice the princess," Martin said to Adam, "then time is not something we can afford to waste." He pointed up the passageway. "This is the quickest, most direct route to the temple." He then glanced at Fenton. "And the treasure."

"What's your game, Conrad?" the river boat captain said. "You bring us here to save time, then you tell us we can't go this way?"

"I never said we couldn't got his way. I said death awaits those who go this way."

Adam saw a hard, cold light fill Captain Fenton's eyes, saw his thick hand drift to the hilt of the jadeite dagger sucked in his belt. "Speak English you little bastard," he said, his voice low and menacing.

Adams mind raced. "Traps! He means there are traps."

Martin nodded. "That would be my guess."

Fenton's eyes narrowed.

The three of them turned their gazes upon the passageway with a newfound respect exceeding its merely artistic merits.

Fenton pointed to Jasper, still perched on Adam's shoulder. "Send the monkey."

"What? No." Adam said. Jasper chirped uneasily.

"Then you go," Fenton insisted.

"Fine."

Martin placed a hand on Adam's shoulder. "Be careful."

Adam smiled and stepped to threshold of the passageway. He studied the friezes but had no honest ideas as to what they portrayed much less what secrets they might conceal. He looked as the starry ceiling and the identically painted floor. He was looking for something, anything in their heavenly depictions, and then he saw it. A difference. An omission to be precise.

"Look," he said to the others. "There are missing elements on the ceiling. See?" He pointed to the floor. "See that double star? Now look directly above it. It's missing." He then pointed to a comet with a serpent's head. "That shooting star has no counterpart on the ceiling either."

Martin nodded proudly. "A pathway through the stars to the *Temple of Heaven*. Well done, Adam.

Fenton removed his skipper's cap and scratched his head. "What if he's wrong?"

But Adam was confident that he was correct. Well, ninety-five percent confident anyway. "Let's find out," he said, and stepped toward the double-star.

29
CORRIDOR OF THE HEAVENS

Step by step, torch in hand, Adam quickly moved up the *Corridor of the Heavens,* making certain to step only upon those motifs with an omitted counterpart above; double-star, comet, sun, comet, crescent moon, etc. and *Death* had not come to greet them.

He wondered what manner of trap a misstep might spring upon them.

They were a good hundred feet up the passageway when they came to a smooth wall upon which was painted a spiraling cosmos.

"What's this, a dead end?" Fenton glared accusingly at Martin.

Martin's long gray beard swayed as he shook his head emphatically. "No. It can't be."

"Well, it sure as hell looks like it to me," Fenton growled.

Adam held his torch higher, examining the fresco. "It's a door."

Visibly relieved, Martin stepped to Adam's side. "It's a puzzle."

Captain Fenton shook his head in frustration. "Which is it, a door, or a puzzle?"

"Both," replied Adam and Martin as one.

Before the river boat captain could say anything more, Adam said, "See here?" He traced a faint line around a painted sun. "Each of the heavenly objects in the picture are painted on fitted stones." Even as he spoke, Adam could envision the stones being pressed like buttons.

"Like buttons," Martin said, echoing his thoughts.

Still, Adam hesitated to test his theory.

Impatient, Fenton said, "So how do you open it?"

From somewhere back down the passageway, deep in the stone walls, something clunked heavily, followed by a deep scraping, grating sound that vibrated through the floor.

Sounding uncharacteristically nervous, Fenton said, "What was that? What's going on?" He looked accusingly at Adam. "Did you push something?"

"No! Of course not."

They looked back to the beginning of the carved and painted corridor where a massive block of stone dropped from the ceiling. It was nearly as wide as the passageway itself; only inches separated it from the ceiling and wall on either side.

"We're trapped," said Martin woefully.

Fenton shook his head. "We might be able to shove it back down the corridor until we can squeeze around it."

A series loud, sharp clanks echoed up the hall, two by two. Clang-clang! Clang-clang! Clang-clang! The massive stone block began to inch forward.

Adam saw the reason at once. "The wall segments are rotating. They're pushing the block forward until the next segments catch it and push it forward."

It was clear to all that, eventually, the huge block of stone would reach them and crush them against the painted door if they failed to open it.

"Do something!" Fenton yelled.

Adam turned back to the wall. Although arranged in a spiral pattern, the images were the same as those painted on the floor and ceiling. As he regarded them it occurred to Adam that there might never had been any danger in stepping anywhere upon the floor. The danger was in reaching the end of the passage where they now stood.

He looked back at the advancing block. It had already covered half the distance to them. He looked away and focused on the wall again.

Think, he told himself. *Think.*

And then his gaze alighted on a double-star. *A double-star.* "That's it!" he exclaimed.

His father leaned close. "What? What is it?"

Rather than reply, Adam simply began to depress motifs. "Double-star, comet, sun, comet, crescent moon…"

Martin grinned behind his bushy mustache. "Yes! Yes! That's it, Adam! You've figured it out!"

Fenton pointed toward the approaching block. "Then do something! It's only ten feet away!"

Adam paused. He couldn't remember the sequence. He glanced back.

"Eight feet!" Fenton cried out.

Adam looked at the floor, then the ceiling between them and the relentless stone. He saw the omits.

"Six feet!"

Adam ignored Fenton's running commentary. "Full moon, double-tailed comet!" Much of the nearest sequence was already lost to sight, he prayed that he hadn't missed anything. He turned his back upon the grating block.

"Four feet!"

Adam could almost feel the press of the stone. Jasper screeched in his ear!

Adam Punched the last two motifs, gritted his teeth, and squeezed his eyes shut.

Everything fell silent. The three of them breathed a collective sigh of relief.

The painted wall began to retract into the side of the passageway.

Fenton slapped him on the back. "You did it, you son of a bitch! You actually did it."

Adam's heart was still racing and sweat still beaded his forehead, but he managed a shaky smile.

The way ahead was a flight of red stone steps. Martin advised caution, but Adam could almost feel the clock ticking for Atziri. Time was running out. He planted a foot on the first step. Nothing. Then the next. Nothing.

"Just stairs," he said. "Seems safe enough."

They continued on up, slowly at first, then, as quickly as an ounce of caution would allow.

At a landing, the stairs switched back 180 degrees, continuing up at the same steep angle. Anxiety hung thick in the air and Adam wasn't sure what worried him most; the thought of yet another booby trap, or confronting at least seven or eight armed Ixinta warriors. It wasn't the first time that he missed his father's old revolver and he was certain it would not be the last.

Adam briefly switched the war club to his left hand in order to wipe the sweat from the palm of his right. It was then that he noticed the faint sounds drifting down from above. He stopped and the others did likewise. "Do you hear that? It sounds like music."

Captain Fenton cupped a hand to one ear and frowned. "Sounds like a bunch of drunks carrying on at the Anaconda."

Martins face grew fearful. "Listen. Trumpets, rattles, ocarinas, and tunkul drums... it's the music of the Sacrifice."

"Atziri," was all Adam said and then he was off, caution be damned, taking the steps two and three at a time.

His father and Fenton followed, calling after him to wait. But the waiting was over. If anything were to happen to Atziri...

30

IN THE TEMPLE OF THE JAGUAR KING

Underfoot, Adam felt another volcanic tremor, but he paid it no heed. He felt the humid touch of the evening air before he reached the top of the stairs. He slowed, then stopped as his rational self reawakened. The drone of rattles, the blare of trumpets, and the thumping of drums were a deafening dirge of terror, but they would also conceal any sounds of their approach.

His father and Fenton caught up with him then.

"Don't do that again," the river boat captain snapped, sounding less self-assured than usual.

Firelight filled the stairwell above them, flickering in time to the ominously hypnotic music.

The three men crept to the top steps and peered out onto a scene *Dante's Inferno*. From their vantage point, in the darker recesses of the temple, the view before them was of the surrounding mountains; black against the red ember glow of the western sky. The temple, perched atop the colossal pyramid, faced away from the ruins of the abandoned city on the plateau.

The foremost mountain was the volcano whose restlessness had been felt off and on since Matthis' escape on the river.

Black smoke rose from the crater in a coiling, serpentine plume. Below the crater, perhaps a quarter of the way down from the peak, a lava-fall oozed from a pitch black hole like a festering wound. The bright orange flow of molten rock plunged from sight between the volcano and the Yanaro plateau.

On the outer edge of the temple floor was a jaguar altar. Carved from stone and painted red, it was also stained black with the blood of untold numbers of human sacrifices. To either side of the altar were seated the warrior-acolytes, musical instruments in hand, instruments of war near to hand. In the center of the temple, three figures loomed over the sacrificial altar. They were dressed in red waist wraps hedl in place by broad belts. Over their bare shoulders they wore a type of feathered jacket draped with ribbons.

Adam noticed all of this within a moment, but there was no sign of, Atziri.

Fenton looked to Martin. "Where is the bloody damned treasure, Conrad?" he hissed.

Before the elder Conrad could answer, the sound of a commotion near the left side of the altar drew their attention. Simon McHenry, bruised, bloodied, and bound, struggled against his Ixinta captors as they propelled him toward the altar.

"They're going to sacrifice him," Adam observed aloud. He knew they had to do something to save the man, but where was Atziri? He was reluctant to act without first knowing where she was.

"Like hell they are," Fenton snarled and drew the jadeite dagger.

Adam pushed Fenton's arm down. "Wait," he said. "You rush out there and you'll get us all killed."

"Get your hand off me and get out of my way," Fenton snarled.

"Weren't you the one who wrote Matthis and McHenry off, saying 'they new the risks'?"

"I never said they deserved to be butchered."

Martin Conrad, plucked Jasper from Adam's shoulder. "We won't let that happen," he said. "But we need a plan."

Adam agreed. His mind raced through several scenarios. None of them ended well.

McHenry woeful "No! No! No!" could be heard above the atonal music. His captors forced him face up upon the altar. They stretched out his arms and legs and began to tie them to four stone pillars positioned at the corners of the altar.

Adam looked at Fenton. "I, I've got nothing."

"Then we just rush them, throw as many over the edge as we can before they even realize we're here."

The High Priest had begun to chant, in a deep and droning type of throat singing.

Adam nodded. "I'll rush the group on the left, you go for the ones on the right."

Fenton smiled grimly. "Fine by me. I…"

There came an explosion of voices behind them. They turned just as half a dozen Ixinta swarmed up the stairs at them. The sprung trap must have alerted them to their presence, Adam realized, but he had no time to wonder where the warriors had come from or how they had gotten behind them.

He caught the first warrior-acolyte across his painted face with the war club. The man spun backward into his companions.

Fenton planted a foot in the face of the first Ixinta to reach him, sending the, warrior tumbling back down the steps.

The music had ceased, only to be replaced shouts of surprise and anger.

"We're surrounded," Martin gulped when the Ixinta did not press the attack.

The High Priest locked eyes with Adam and a cold smile curled his lips back, exposing teeth chiseled to points. His face was painted in red and green and his ears were weighed down by heavy jade spools. The High Priest's visage was frightful in the extreme but not for any of these things.

It was his eyes; eyes so black they could have been carved from obsidian, like the dagger in his hands. The High Priest pointed the black blade at Adam and spat a series of harsh sounding commands to his servants.

Immediately, Adam and the others were set upon from both sides. Martin was slammed back against the wall, while Jasper, hooting and screeching, tumbled clear of the melee.

Two Ixinta sprang at Adam like wild beasts. He lashed out at them with the war club, but they easily avoided his clumsy swing. The next thing he knew, the club was stripped from his grip and a hail of fists and feet rained down upon him. As he collapsed on the cold stone under the weight of his assailants, he glimpsed the river boat captain.

Fenton, even as he was swarmed by Ixinta, managed to sink the jadeite dagger into the stomach of one of his attackers. He slashed at a second but a war club sent his bloodied green blade skittering away across the temple floor just as Jasper had.

31
SACRIFICES

In all of the chaos, Yaotyl, the High Priest had remained standing at the altar, turning in place only to track Adam and the others as they were dragged to a tight rank of ornately caved stone pillars. His malevolent black eyes watched approvingly as they were backed against the pillars and tied to them.

Adam fumed, desperate for some sign of Atziri.

"Next time, I make the plan," Fenton growled.

"This was your plan, remember?" Adam replied.

Fenton's expression soften. "Oh, yeah. I guess it was."

Martin, tied to the pillar to Adam's right, said, "It doesn't matter. We're doomed." He lifted his bearded chin toward the altar.

Yaotyl waited until they were all looking at him then he looked to Martin. "Su'tan!" he said, in a hard, flinty voice.

Martin inclined his head to Adam and, without taking his eyes from the priest, began to translate. "Thank you for gracing this most holy of holy ceremonies. We are grateful for your sacrifice. Your roll in this momentous occasion will be recorded for all ages. Your memories will live forever."

Fenton spat. "Tell him if I'm going to die, I want to see the blasted treasure first!"

The High Priest's head snapped to Martin. "Su'tan!"

Martin spoke, apparently translating Fenton's words.

Yaotyl laughed mirthlessly. The two holy men flanking him laughed in kind. The High Priest slashed the air with is obsidian dagger and the silence followed.

He stepped slowly down from the altar and, dagger raised before him, crossed to Fenton. The river boat captain remained stoic but his skin had turned gray. Yaotyl placed the tip of the blade against Fenton's chest. He glanced at Martin. "Su'tan," he said and began to speak.

Martin translated. "Do not be so hasty to behold the *Treasure of the Jaguar King*. Because when you do see it, and you will, it will be as the life fades from your eyes."

As Yaotyl turned back to the altar, Adam called after him. "Where is Atziri."

The High Priest stopped in his tracks but did not look back. "Ah'zee'ree."

Adam noticed Yaotyl tighten his grip on the sacrificial dagger. The High Priest strode back to the altar.

"Where is she?" Adam demanded. "Where is Atziri!"

His plea fell upon deaf ears.

The warrior-acolytes took up their instruments and resumed their chaotic, spine tingling dirge.

The High Priest had again turned to the grisly business at hand. He looked down at McHenry, still tied down upon the altar.

"Captain! McHenry called as Yaotyl and the two other priests resumed their throat singing chant, every word more minacious than the last.

Yaotyl raised high the black dagger.

"Captain! Do something!" McHenry shrieked.

Adam could see the torment in Fenton's face, but there was nothing anyone could do.

Simon McHenry screamed as the obsidian blade flash downward like a bolt of black lightning. It drove deep into his chest, ending his scream as it ended his life.

Yaotyl's companions crowded close like feasting vultures. A moment later they stepped back with blood soaked hands. Yaotyl raised high McHenry's heart and called out to the smoldering volcano.

The two lesser priests severed the ropes that bound McHenry's corpse to the altar. They then lifted his body and hurled over the precipice.

Yaotyl tossed McHenry's heart into the flames of a nearby brazier.

Adam felt like vomiting in wake of the horrid spectacle, but he knew that the horrors were far from over.

With a serpentine fluidity, the High Priest, Yaotyl, pointed the sacrificial dagger to a dark, unlit alcove of the temple. The pair of servant priests hurried into the gloom, emerging a moment later, dragging Ed Matthis with them.

Adam stared into the blackness, but the darkness of the alcove was impenetrable. Was Atziri held prisoner there as well?

Like McHenry before him. Matthis was brought before the altar. He saw the fresh blood pooled upon upon it and his legs buckled. The priests held him up while Yaotyl concluded whatever evil he had been chanting.

Matthis saw them, and instantly implored Fenton for help. "Charles, talk to them. Offer them something, anything, in exchange for our lives!"

"There's nothing we can do, Ed. So stop your whining. Die with dignity." Fenton's words might have sounded harsh, but Adam knew they were born of helpless frustration.

"You're a bigger bastard than even I imagined," Matthis choked as tears began to flow.

The High Priest elegantly gestured Matthis to the altar, as though bidding the artist to recline and relax. The pair of priests propping Matthis up, forced him back upon the stone jaguar and proceeded to tie him down.

Adam strained against his bonds. It was no use. If only... He glance down and found Jasper tugging at the hem of his pants leg with one tiny hand. With the other, he cradled the jadeite dagger that had been knocked from Fenton's hands.

The Capuchin monkey was like an answered prayer. " Give me the knife. Put the knife in my hand. My hand Jasper. You see?" He wiggled his fingers to direct Jasper's attention to his hands.

Jasper began to clime the stone pillar. "That's it Jasper, good boy."

The trumpets rose in volume and pitch, the tunkul drums became thunderous. Impossibly, the glow of the lava-fall from the side of the volcano seemed to brighten in response.

Adam glanced back as Jasper placed the dagger in his hands. "Good Jasper." Adam trained his eyes ahead, watching Yaotyl, his attendant priests, and the warrior-acolytes furiously playing their ritualistic music. As he watched, he worked the keen edge of the carved jadeite blade against the ropes that secured him to the pillar by his wrists.

The High Priest bellowed something to the volcano across the narrow valley. The obsidian dagger was a blur as it came to rest deep in Matthis' chest.

At that exact same moment, Adam's bonds parted before the jadeite dagger.

Adam stayed put, arms wrapped around the pillar behind himself as the bloody ceremony played out. His thoughts reeled. It would be him against every Ixinta in the temple, eight at least. He needed help. He wouldn't have time to free both his father and Fenton. As much as it pained him, right now, he needed the burly river boat captain more.

Still standing as though bound, Adam was staring at Yaotyl as the music ended and the High Priest turned to face him.

Yaotyl's black gaze shifted to Martin. "Su'tan!" he ordered, and then began to speak at length and Martin translated.

"It is time for the Ixinta, the true Yanaro, to assume their rightful place on the *Jaguar Throne*! Behold! The night's sacrifices have stirred the spirit of Yanarotequal! In moments, the blood of the once lost princess will return sight to the eyes of, Yanarotequal. Then, Yanarotequal will see his true children and the world and everything within it will once again be theirs!"

"You're insane," Fenton spat.

Yaotyl's face was split by his sharp toothed smile. He then spoke to the other priests who then scurried away like insects. Yaotyl stretched forth his left hand. The blood splattered jade bracelet and rings that adorned it, glinted in the coppery light of the braziers and torches.

The two priests returned. One of them carrying something concealed beneath a thick red cloth. Yaotyl never took his eyes off Adam and the others as his priests removed the cloth to reveal a pair of trapiche emeralds, each the size of an apple.

"Holy Moses! Do you see what I see?" Fenton rasped. "Martin, you were right. We were all right!"

To his right, Martin Conrad only sobbed. Adam knew they were not tears of joy or vindication. They were tears of pure and bitter sorrow.

Yaotyl issued another command and the pair of lesser priests hurried to comply.

The High Priest's sweaty skin glistened like wet copper in lava-glow and firelight. He turned toward the *Jaguar Altar* and stared out into the night, where only the radiant orange column of the lava-fall was visible in the blackness. He raised both arms; obsidian dagger in one hand, the *Treasure of the Jaguar King* in the other.

There was a disturbance near the far, dark alcove. The lesser priests reappeared and Adam's world drained of sound and blurred at the edges, until only one thing remained.

Atziri!

32
TREASURE OF THE JAGUAR KING

Atziri.

Against the blood soaked horrors of the evening, against the hellishness of Yaotyl the High Priest, Atziri had never been more resplendent. But there was a terror in her beauty, ancient and timeless, that Adam struggled to rectify with the gentle, angelic woman that he loved.

Her long black hair was pulled high upon the back of her head, wrapped in jade and gold headdress. A profusion of arm-length, iridescent quetzal feathers, protruded from the top of the headdress.

Jade, gold, and silver accouterments – bracelets, pendants, rings, and anklets – the trappings of royalty adorned her. She wore only a large, full-length, pure white *huipil,* with blue edging.

The world came back into focus.

"Atziri!" Adam called out to her, but she stared straight ahead as though in a trance. *They've drugged her,* Adam realized. The lesser priests, each guiding her by one arm, directed her toward the altar.

Adam's heart began to pound furiously. He resisted the urge to rush to her aid. He knew that if he had even the slightest hope of saving her, he needed to free Captain Fenton first.

As Atziri was laid across the altar of sacrifice, the High Priest turned is black, evil gaze once more to Adam and smiled like the Devil incarnate. "Az'ee'ree." he taunted. Then turned once more to the business at hand.

The music rose again and Yaotyl began his throat singing chant.

Now! Adam thought. He cast away his severed bonds and rush to the backside of Fenton's pillar.

Captain Fenton blinked in amazement. "What the hell?" he said as Adam cut the leather bonds. "Hey, that's my knife? How did you...?"

Adam pointed to Jasper who had returned to Martin's side, then handed Fenton the jadeite blade. "Your original plan?"

Fenton nodded. "Works for me."

And then it began. Adam was upon the first of the three warrior-acolytes on Yaotyl's left. He slammed against the drummer, sending the him and his tunkul drum over the temple's cliff-like edge. He snatched up the warrior's bladed club and rushed the second before anyone realized what was happening.

As Adam clashed with his targets, the river boat captain swept past the three priest and Atziri from behind. By then, he had lost the element of surprise. The three warrior-acolytes on Yaotyl's right were alerted as Adam sent his first target to his death. They cast aside their instruments and reached for their weapons. Fenton never slowed. He powered into the first warrior-acolyte like a train. Without stopping, he drove all three over the precipice in one clean sweep.

Adam was not quite the locomotive that Fenton was. The second musician was quick. Startled, he hurled his trumpet at Adam and snatched up the war-club he'd kept at the ready. Even as Adam ducked the wind instrument the warrior-acolyte's club came whistling toward his head. Adam parried the strike, but by then third man was now on his feet, ready to fight.

Adam swept low and the obsidian blades of the war-club broke the calf of the second man. Yowling in pain, the warrior-acolyte fell back, collided with his companion. The third warrior never hesitated. He simply shoved his wounded brethren over the edge, clearing a path strait for Adam.

Beyond the approaching warrior, Adam saw Fenton turn back toward the altar but then he also saw one of the lesser priests turn to confront him.

As Adam hefted his club, he realized that his slowly circling opponent was trying to back him toward the drop off. Aware of the need to end things quickly, Adam lunged his enemy. The warrior-acolyte's eyes widened, surprised by Adam's sudden move. They clashed then; the stone blades of their war-clubs sparking as they collided.

With his free hand, Adam caught the warrior's club wielding arm at the wrist, only to have warrior -acolyte do likewise to him. They struggled then, each trying to dislodge the other's weapon, wrestling ever closer to the precipice and the volcanic lake far below.

The bracelet on the other man's wrist kept rolling under Adam's grip, making it difficult to fully restrain the warrior's arm. He was losing his hold and losing ground as the Ixinta warrior began to slowly inch him toward a molten oblivion.

"Captain! A little help would be nice!" As he called out, he glimpsed Fenton disposing of the last of Yaotyl's assisstant priests, already eyeing the High Priest who still held the massive trapiche emeralds in his hand. Adam knew it wasn't Yaotyl, but the fabled *Treasure of the Jaguar King* that river boat captain was fixated on.

With no help from Fenton, Adam acted in desperation. He raised his foot and planted it with all his might in his adversary's chest. The warrior-acolyte gasped and staggered backward.

Adam rushed after him, swept his war-club back, preparing to land a decisive strike, but he drew up short, stopped by the sudden expression on other man's ornamented face.

The man's dark eyes practically bulged from their sockets, his mouth opened wide, voicing a silent scream. And then Adam saw the cause.

Yaotyl.

The black point of the High Priest's sacrificial blade jutted out from the warrior-acolyte's chest. Yaotyl whispered savagely into the dying man's ear. Even without Martin to translate, Adam was certain the man had died for failure in Yaotyl's black eyes.

Then Fenton was upon the High Priest. He plunged the jadeite dagger between the Ixinta holy man's shoulders and ripped the emeralds from his hand.

A snarl of rage broke from the High Priest's sharp-toothed mouth. He ripped the lavish, though cumbersome headdress from his head and wheeled around to face Fenton. Marveling at the *Treasure of the Jaguar King* now in his possession, the river boat captain never even saw Yaotyl as the High Priest ran his black blade through his neck.

"No!" Adam rushed forward, but he was too late. Charles Fenton, captain of *la Tortuga*, staggered backward toward the edge of the temple overlooking the volcanic lake.

The High Priest, realizing what he had done, stretch out his free hand toward Fenton.

Fenton teetered on the edge, his shirt bathed in his own blood. He looked at past Yaotyl, raised the invaluable *Eyes of the Jaguar*, and smiled at Adam in pitiful triumph. Then he slipped over the edge, taking the *Treasure of the Jaguar King* with him.

The High Priest let forth a howl a pure anguish. Chest heaving with rage, sacrificial dagger in hand, he turned to face Adam. Between them, lying on her back, tied down upon the jaguar altar, Atziri was waking from her daze. As she stirred, she began to struggle against her restraints.

Yaotyl, still seething with rage shifted his focus from Adam to Atziri. He crouched low, uttering what could only be curses and rushed toward her, dagger ready to strike.

Adam too was on the move, but the High Priest was closer to Atziri. Too close.

Adam made a hasty Sign of the Cross and slung the the war-club like a sidearm baseball pitch. The bladed club spun through the air.

Just as Yaotyl raised the dagger to end Atziri's life, the war-club caught him in the midsection, just under the ribs. The obsidian dagger fell from his hand, shattering on the stone floor. He staggered once, then fell to his knees, dead.

Adam rushed to the altar and with a shard of the black blade, quickly cut Atziri's bonds. She slid from the altar into his arms.

"You came for me," she said.

Adam smiled. "I love you, what else could I do?"

EPILOGUE

Adam sat at the tiller of the *Moonflower* as they steamed down the *Rio Lagarto* toward Mar Azul. He was bone weary; they all were. He felt as though he could sleep for days. The canopy kept the brunt of the sun at bay, but it did little about the heat. Which only compounded his sense of exhaustion.

Atziri, still wearing the full-length huipil of the Ixinta, was sitting sideways, drowsing on the bench next to him, her back against his arm, her feet upon the port side gunwale.

Jasper sat on his other side, picking absently at the fur of his tail.

Martin Conrad, now dressed in an extra set of Adam's clothes, sat in the bow. In one had, he held a small shaving mirror. In the other, Adam's straight razor. He turned his face from side to side, examining himself in the tiny mirror. Apparently satisfied, he rinsed the razor in the river.

He made his way aft and sat on the starboard side bench. "I feel like I've traveled twenty years backward in time," he said. He looked away, out across the easy flow of the *Lagarto*. "If only I really could."

Adam could hear the sense of loss and regret in his father's voice. "We can't change the past, Dad. What matters is today and tomorrow."

Martin sighed. "I never stopped thinking about, or your mother. I spent so much time imaging what might have been if only we had given up looking for the treasure, if only we had listened to Father Kirby."

Adam felt a knot in his throat at the mention of the priest. "He was good man."

Martin smiled. "I believe so. He seems to have done a good job raising you."

Adam laughed lightly. "Me and Atziri; and I can't say we made it easy for him."

They fell into a comfortable silence for a time. Jasper, having lost interest in preening his tail hopped off the bench and began snooping in the supplies under the bench.

At length, Adam said to Martin, "So what comes next?"

His father seemed to consider his answer. "Well, if you and Atziri are serious about starting your business, I thought maybe I could work for you."

Adam brightened at the idea. He hadn't sure if his father's plan might be to stay, or to return to Michigan. Working together would let them get to know each other, to become the family they were meant to be. "I think that's a great idea," he said.

"It should be a unanimous decision," Martin said. He nodded toward Atziri, who was still napping against Adam. "Let's hear what she has to say about it when she wakes."

"I'm awake," Atziri said languidly without opening her eyes. "I think it's a grand idea."

Adam smiled. "Well then I guess it's settled."

Jasper climbed back onto the bench next to Adam and began to pat down his pockets, looking for something to eat. Being quite accustomed to the little beggar, Adam only half payed attention to him until he began to fidget with the button on Adam's pants pocket.

The pendant! In all pf the excitement, Adam had all but forgotten the golden necklace.

The Capuchin monkey hooted irritably as Adam shooed him away. "Nothing there for you, buster." He nudged Atziri. "But you on the other hand..."

She sat up, curious. "What?"

"I have something for you." He drew the pendant from his pocket and handed it to Atziri.

Her dark eyes opened wide. She took it and cradled it in her palms for several moment before clutching it to her heart. She smiled even as tears flowed down her cheeks. "How did... Where did you..."

Flustered by her emotional reaction, Adam stammered. "I, I found it under the waterfall when I was chasing you and Matthis. I thought you might like it."

"I do like it, more than you know," she said as she threw her arms around him. "It was my grandmother's."

She sat back, and held the pendant up for them to see. The necklace was fashioned in the ornate, disk shape of a stylized Yanaro calendar stone. Among the motifs, an emerald eyed jaguar chased, and was chased by, a ruby-eyed spider.

After their recent adventure, Adam now recognized that the imagery represented the eternal battle between the Yanaro and the Ixinta.

"May I?" Martin asked.

Atziri handed him the pendant. He studied it, turning it over in his hands. "Curious," he said.

"How so?" Adam asked.

"Well, for one thing, the eyes of the jaguar are trapiche emeralds, starred emeralds, just like the Treasure of the Jaguar King. Exceedingly small, mind you, but trapiche all the same. But," he continued, his brow rising for emphasis, "that's not the most curious thing."

He turned the pendant around to show them the back face. It looked much like the first in that it was fashioned as a golden calendar stone, but gone were the jaguar and the spider. In their place was the image of a feathered serpent, encircling and emerald and a ruby.

"What does it mean?" Atziri asked.

Martin shrugged. "Who knows," he said and handed the pendant back to her. "But I think we can all agree that it is a beautiful piece, quite a treasure in its own right."

Atziri smiled and, as she slipped the necklace around her neck, the hair on the nape of Adam's neck prickled to life. Whatever the serpent motif signified, he knew in his gut that the pendant was more than just a pretty little treasure with great sentimental value.

THE ADVENTURE CONTINUES IN "TREASURE OF THE SPIDER KING"

THE ADVENTURE CONTINUES IN
"TREASURE OF THE SPIDER KING"

ABOUT THE AUTHOR

J. A. Johnson is the author of the epic fantasy series, "Dragons West", as well as "Legends of the Coast", a young adult fantasy for all ages. He is also the author of, "Treasure of the Jaguar King", the first in a series of Indiana Jones-style adventures.

With K. G.McAbee, he is the co-creator and co-author of the "NEREUS PROJECT Deep Sea Thriller Series". He is also the creator of the drawing tutorial video series, "Drawing with Cheesecake the Cat".

He lives with his wife and son in Upstate South Carolina where he is currently working on multiple new projects.

www.evanationstudios.com

www.ingramcontent.com/pod-product-compliance
Lightning Source LLC
Chambersburg PA
CBHW021405150726
47989CB00005B/2407